The proposal: An all-expense-paid vacation
The catch: You have to spy on your wealthy
benefactor's bachelor son, Craig Derring.

The proposal: Share close quarters with sexy
Craig
The catch: A prim-and-proper woman like
you doesn't do that kind of thing!

The proposal: Marriage!
The catch: Craig hasn't exactly asked. But
your father-in-law-to-be is counting on it....

Dear Reader,

Well, I'm no heiress—would that I were! But after entering the dating fray, I can see why Shannon Powell, heroine of Maris Soule's *Heiress Seeking Perfect Husband,* would try a new tack: telling a reporter exactly what she's looking for. Of course, I doubt I'd get any letters as wonderful as those Shannon gets from "Cyrano." I also doubt my letter writer would turn out to be my handsome, in-love-with-me-for-forever chauffeur. Of course, maybe that's because I don't have a chauffeur, and because the men who drive me home are more likely to think Cyrano comes from Syria than that he's a lover straight out of literature. But that's another story!

And so is this: Lori Herter's *Me? Marry You?* This is the latest in her MILLION-DOLLAR MARRIAGES miniseries, and it's a winner. I mean, really, who could turn down an all-expense-paid vacation with *the* most gorgeous hunk? Not Penelope Grey, even though she knows the hunk's over-the-top-wealthy father is angling to make a match between them. In fact, before too long, Penelope is hoping gorgeous Craig Derring will fall right in line with those incredibly romantic plans.

So enjoy both of this month's books, and don't forget to come back next month for more great reading about meeting, dating—and marrying!—Mr. Right.

Leslie Wainger
Senior Editor and Editorial Coordinator

Please address questions and book requests to:
Silhouette Reader Service
U.S.: 3010 Walden Ave., P.O. Box 1325, Buffalo, NY 14269
Canadian: P.O. Box 609, Fort Erie, Ont. L2A 5X3

LORI HERTER

Me? Marry You?

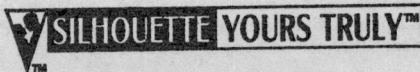

▼ SILHOUETTE YOURS TRULY™

Published by Silhouette Books

America's Publisher of Contemporary Romance

To my husband, Jerry

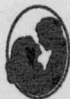

SILHOUETTE BOOKS

ISBN 0-373-52035-2

ME? MARRY *YOU?*

This edition published by arrangement with Harlequin Books S.A.

® and TM are trademarks of Harlequin Books S.A., used under license.
Trademarks indicated with ® are registered in the United States Patent
and Trademark Office, the Canadian Trade Marks Office and in other
countries.

Printed in U.S.A.

About the author

The idea that opposites attract has fascinated people for ages, and it always makes for a good romance. When I married my husband, Jerry, twenty-three years ago, I thought I was marrying someone very similar to me—same socioeconomic background, same religion, similar tastes in movies and music. Most of all, we seemed to be on the same wavelength. We both even shared an interest in geology and rock collecting. In fact, we were so much alike, I used to worry that the marriage might get boring!

After a few years, however, it became clear we were opposites on a fairly important issue: travel. Jerry has a sense of adventure and I don't. While I'm taking a white-knuckle flight, he's sitting next to me on the plane relaxed and happy as a clam that our long-awaited vacation has finally begun. He likes to snorkle, take scenic helicopter rides over steep cliffs, glaciers and volcanoes, climb to high places and stand an inch from the edge to look at the view. I prefer to be on dry land as close to sea level as possible.

In *Me?* Marry *You?* I had the opportunity to laugh at myself through my heroine, Penelope. Her phobias and foibles are based on my own. And if Craig seems unusually patient with her, it's because his tolerant nature is based on my husband's.

Hope you enjoy Craig and Penelope's romance!

Books by Lori Herter

Silhouette Yours Truly

Listen Up, Lover
*How Much Is That Couple in the Window?
*Blind-Date Bride
*<u>Me?</u> Marry <u>You?</u>

*Million-Dollar Marriages

Silhouette Romance

Loving Deception #344

Silhouette Shadows

The Willow File #28

Silhouette Books

Silhouette Shadows Short Story Collection 1993
"The Phantom of Chicago"

1

Jasper Derring picked up a colorful postcard from the pile of mail just delivered by the mailman. The card showed palm trees swaying over a white sand beach with a sailboat in the distance. Jasper knew before he turned the card over that it came from his eldest son. The corner of his mouth quirked as he read the breezy, familiar handwriting on the reverse side.

> Greetings, Folks!
> I'm good. Hope everything's copacetic on your side of the planet. Have new digs and a new phone number—555-2123. Same area code, same P.O. box, same town, same island, same zip. Wanted to let you know.
>
> Aloha, Craig

Jasper's wife, Bea, walked into the sunroom where Jasper was sitting on a wicker couch. "Is that today's mail already?" she asked, eyeing the stack beside him. "Postman must be ahead of schedule. Just bills and catalogs, as usual?"

In a dour humor, he held up the card in his hand. "No, we received a special missive from Craig."

Bea sat beside him on the couch and took the card. "Oh," she said with interest as she read the note. "He's moved!" She smiled. "Doesn't say exactly where—isn't that like him? Well, it was nice he took the time to let us know how to reach him."

"Wasn't it, though?" Jasper said in a sarcastic voice. "Must have taken him all of ten seconds to write the card, another second to lick the stamp, and he probably dropped it in some mailbox on his way to the closest beer party."

"Jasper," she chided. "When he flew in for Charles's wedding, he told me he'd cut back on all the partying he used to do. I had the feeling he was finally settling down. And now he's got a new place."

"Maybe he was evicted from the old one," Jasper muttered.

"Don't be such a grumble-puss."

"He's our eldest, Bea. I've got a right! I had such high expectations for him. He's so bright, but he never applies himself. He's thirty-four now. Must be the oldest beach 'boy' on the Big Island—or all of Hawaii, for that matter."

Bea carefully retied the loosened ribbon at the nape of her neck, catching her long gray hair back, George Washington-style. "It's because you had such high expectations that he left Chicago," she reminded him. "You wanted him to follow in your footsteps, and he wanted to create his own path." Her ribbon neatly adjusted, she turned to her husband, elbow on the back of the couch. "He made it clear he simply didn't want to be a millionaire's son, running his dad's department store chain. And it was just as well, since Charles turned out to be perfectly suited for that job. Craig seems very happy doing . . . whatever it is he's doing." She waved her hand vaguely. "Running that...that snorkel boat for tourists, or whatever." She scratched her cheek. "I asked him at the wedding if that was still his line of work. His reply was sort of muddled, but I think he said yes."

"Charles's wedding took place over two years ago," Jasper reminded her. "Craig might be sewing grass hula skirts now, for all we know. And chasing them—I'm sure we could bet on that!"

Bea's delicate eyebrows furrowed. "Craig does seem to have gotten more than his share of wild oats, it's true. Of all our children, I confess, I worry about him the most. I hope this new place he's found to live is halfway decent and not in some low rent district."

Jasper exhaled in a snort. "How can we know? Even if I went there to visit him, he'd meet me at our Kona condo and never show me his place. Unless..." he turned to Bea, "maybe if you came along, he'd—"

Bea slid her hand nervously along the waistband of her skirt. "That's such a long plane trip from Chicago," she said, shaking her head. "If it's a bumpy flight, they'd have to carry me off the plane."

"I know," Jasper said, patting her shoulder. Bea had a lifelong problem with motion sickness. Medications and ear patches only made her woozy or too sleepy to function. Damn Craig! Jasper thought, shifting in his seat. Why was he so secretive?

Whenever Jasper had visited Hawaii over the years, Craig always looked good, seemed happy, and had lots of friends, judging by the way people said hello to him wherever they went. Jasper knew Craig had an old catamaran in Kailua-Kona that he used to take tourists snorkeling, because he always took him out on the craft for a few hours. But in Jasper's several visits over the dozen years since Craig had moved to Hawaii, he'd never once offered to show Jasper where he lived, always saying his place was being fumigated, or repaired, or some such excuse.

Jasper took the postcard back from Bea, glanced at the note again, and then absently began tapping the card on the arm of the couch as he became preoccupied with his thoughts. Maybe it was time he gave up hoping his son would ever confide in them. Maybe it was time he did a little investigation on his own. After all, poor Bea shouldn't have to worry so much, and neither should he, at their age. They were Craig's parents—they had a right to know!

Bea eyed him tapping the card as he formed his plans. "What are you thinking, Jasper?"

"Me?" He stopped tapping. "Oh, nothing, Bea." He acted nonchalant, because he knew his wife would never approve of him prying into their son's affairs.

"Nothing? Honest?"

"Of course," he insisted, gazing at her with a look of complete sincerity. "What would I be thinking?"

Bea sighed. "I've lived with you for forty-some years, and I still haven't fathomed all the parameters of your mind. For all I know, you might be thinking of learning to scuba dive, so you can spy on Craig on his boat from underwater."

Jasper shifted his eyes back and forth. Actually, her idea sounded rather inventive, except that he was too old to carry it off. He had a bad heart, too. No, he'd have to hire someone else to do whatever spying needed to be done.

He reached out and tweaked Bea's nose affectionately. "You're beginning to think like me."

"Oh, gosh," she said, looking abashed. "I hope not!"

* * *

Craig Derring walked into the home he'd recently purchased, located in the high, green hills overlooking Kealakekua Bay and Napoopoo Beach on the Kona coast. His employee, Ned Pukui, a sturdily built, black-haired man in his forties, who kept Craig's fleet of catamarans in top repair, was refinishing the kitchen cabinets. The smell of fresh varnish met Craig's nostrils as he walked in.

"How's it going?" he asked Ned. "Looks great!" The old faded wood looked mellow and rich now.

"It's goin' good." Ned took much pride in his craftsmanship.

"Like a beer?" Craig offered, opening the refrigerator.

"Sure!"

Craig handed Ned a beer and took out a cola drink for himself. "I just bought a yacht today, up in Hilo. Thought I'd use it for sunset cruises." He opened the can and took a swig of cola. "Needs to be repainted, though—detailed nicely. I'd like you to put off work here to go do that next week, if you don't mind."

Ned hesitated and opened his can of beer before replying, "Whatever you want." He leaned against the tiled counter and grinned. "Not anxious for me to start refinishing the floors here, eh?"

Craig chuckled. "I'm not looking forward to the mess. I'll probably have to move out for a few nights."

"Be a good idea," Ned agreed. "Can't walk around. Strong fumes while it's drying. But if you're serious about redoing all your wood floors, you shouldn't keep putting it off. Just about everything else on the house is finished."

"Yeah, well . . . I still need you to do the new boat. I'd like to get that in operation in Kailua-Kona for the August swell of tourists. You can take one of the guys with you to help."

"You got it, boss."

Craig knew Ned thought he was procrastinating, and he supposed he was. But he'd gotten used to sleeping in the large master bedroom upstairs with the French doors open onto the lanai and its spectacular view, and the cool night breezes wafting through the room from off the ocean. Sometimes he could even hear the distant waves. He'd never thought he'd want a "dream house," but now that he had one, he hated to give it up, even to refurbish the neglected, aging wood floors.

The house had been the home of a coffee grower and had been built in the 1940s. It had a plantation look to it, with large white pillars across the front, facing the ocean. The home was reached by a private, winding road and was difficult to find—which Craig liked. He was beginning to appreciate solitude.

After college he'd lived for a while on money he'd gotten from his parents as a graduation present, escaping the city life he'd known and getting into the Hawaiian life-style. He'd moved from island to island, exploring, partying, enjoying the beach life, scoping out bikini-clad babes and making friends. When his money ran out after a year and a half, he began living on a shoestring giving private snorkeling excursions off a catamaran he'd bought cheap in Kailua-Kona. It had seen better days, but he'd met Ned, a local handyman, who said he could fix it up like new. Ned did as promised. Soon Craig had more business than he could manage by himself, so he bought a second catamaran and hired a friend to handle that one. Now, after little more than a decade in Hawaii, he had a boat or two in every scenic bay on the Big Island, as well as on Oahu, Maui, and Kauai.

One day about two years ago, Craig's accountant had informed him, barely able to control his excitement, that Craig had become a millionaire. Craig sat in the accountant's office, dumbfounded. "What do you mean?" he'd asked, his mind numb from being up too late partying the night before. The accountant explained that his income had increased to the point where, when he cleared expenses, he had made a million dollars that year. Craig should have been happy, but he wasn't. A millionaire was what his father had wanted him to become.

Craig had been so rebellious in his teenage years and into his twenties that whatever his strong-willed dad wanted for him, Craig wanted exactly the opposite. Since he was the oldest, Jasper had expected him to run Derring Brothers, the family's renowned department store in Chicago. *No way!* Craig had vowed. He wanted to be his own man, not his father's clone.

After completing college to please his mother, Craig had headed directly for the beaches of Hawaii and had never gone back—except very briefly for his brother's wedding. He'd never particularly wanted to become successful, because he didn't want to give his father that satisfaction. Now that he'd become a millionaire despite himself, he hoped to keep the news quiet. Only his accountant and his oldest friends, like Ned, knew for sure, though his company, Sunshine Snorkeling Cruises, had grown so fast, he was beginning to be perceived as successful. He still appeared laid-back and fun-loving, though he no longer stayed out late partying. He had too many responsibilities nowadays.

Sometimes the change in his circumstances troubled Craig. He wondered if he was becoming like his father without knowing it. For example, why had he bought a house?

One afternoon about four months ago he'd been driving back to his old condo in Kailua-Kona—he'd kept the fact that he owned a condo a secret from his parents—after snorkeling at Napoopoo Beach. Somehow he'd taken a wrong turn as he drove inland, up the steep hills. He'd found himself on a narrow road and had had to keep going as there was no place to turn around. Suddenly the thick foliage on either side had opened out onto a green lawn and the most beautiful house he'd ever seen. It looked empty, as if it hadn't been used for years. The next day Craig had asked a real estate friend in town about it. The house hadn't officially been for sale, but when the owner had learned there was an interested buyer who could pay cash, he'd sold it after some bargaining. Craig had argued that the property needed a lot of repair and won his point, getting the stately house with its spectacular view at a steal.

So now Craig found himself not only a millionaire, but the owner of a big house—some might say a mansion—on a prominent overlook by the sea. It bothered him to think how proud his dad would be of him, if he knew. Craig sort of wished he could tell his mother, though. He felt guilty, knowing she probably worried about him.

"Bet I know why you keep putting off having the floors refinished," Ned said, taking a swig of beer after cleaning his brushes in turpentine.

"I'm a procrastinator?" Craig replied.

"No. You like having somebody around, working on the place. When it's finished, you'll be all alone in this big house."

Craig hadn't thought of that. "Nah, I don't mind being alone here."

"A party animal like you?" Ned said with a grin.

"I'm growing to like solitude."

"Yeah, I've noticed lately you leave luaus and get-togethers even before I do. But I've got a family. You're going to come home to these silent rooms." Ned motioned to indicate the expanse of the large kitchen and empty dining room next to it. "You haven't even got much furniture—one old couch in that big living room and a new king-size bed upstairs. Gonna invite some pretty wahine to share it, or what?"

Craig rubbed his nose, slightly irritated. "I don't know. Maybe."

"You haven't had a steady girlfriend in a long time. You don't even chase after babes much nowadays. Tired of sex?"

Craig shot him a give-me-a-break look. "No! Why all these questions?"

Ned shrugged. "I don't think you're happy anymore. Not the way you used to be. You act like you don't exactly know what to do with yourself, you know? You used to be content hanging out, doing nothing."

Craig hated to admit that Ned was right. He had been feeling edgy, or bored, or *something* lately. "I'll get over it."

"Yeah, but how? See, that's the key question. You want to know what I think?"

"How much can I pay you *not* to tell me?" Craig swished the carbonated soda in his can to hide his annoyance.

"Actually, it was my wife who said it the other day," Ned went on obliviously. "She thinks you ought to get married. I believe she's onto something."

Craig had begun to take a sip of his drink and choked. After a cough, he said, "Huh?"

"Married. It's time, man. How old are you?"

"Thirty-four is not old."

"It ain't twenty-four. See, I wouldn't say anything if I saw you still enjoying life and babes and boats the way you did years ago, when you first started hiring me. But you were a carefree kid then. Now you're older. You're getting some wisdom—a little. Your old life doesn't suit you anymore and you're not sure what your new life should be. You're in transition," Ned said, raising his forefinger to make his point. "That's how I'd put it—in transition."

Craig set his can of cola on the counter and exhaled with dour humor. "Maybe so. But where do you see me with a wife in your scheme of things?"

"No, man, it's your life and *your* scheme. I'm just pointing out the signs I see. You bought this house. Shows you have a yen to set down some roots. But are you going to be a hermit here? I don't see it. Not you."

"I won't be a hermit. I'll be out working all day, dealing with my employees, with tourists. This is a restful place to come to at day's end."

Ned nodded. "But how restful? You going to be celibate here? Meditate, like in a monastery?"

"Why is my sex life so important to you?"

Ned began to put his brushes away in a wooden case, as if needing a pause before answering. Finally he looked up. "Okay, I'll be straight with you. You've always been real great to work for, and I've appreciated that. You don't hassle me, you're true to your word, and . . . you *used* to be easygoing."

"I'm not anymore?" Craig asked, puzzled.

"You're getting...I don't know...antsy. You keep changing your mind. Like today. First you wanted me to finish the house. Now you want me to quit and go work on the new boat. Tomorrow, you'll want something else again. It's hard for me to make plans. My wife will be a mite annoyed when I tell her I have to go over to Hilo, when she was counting on me being home next week."

That's the problem with wives, Craig thought but didn't say. "Sorry, I didn't realize. I can have someone bring the boat around to Kailua. How's that?"

Ned's face brightened. "Yeah, okay. Thanks. That'll help a lot. I don't mean to complain, but you get my drift? You've got no life now. Get one! Sure a wife is a ball and chain—you can look at it that way. But they're convenient, too. You don't have to go out looking for women. Easy sex. She might even cook. You get tired of restaurant food. It's nice to eat at home. And then the kids come. You won't be lonely the rest of your life."

Craig began feeling really irked. Angry, in fact. It took a moment to realize why. "You're beginning to remind me of my father," he told Ned. "He'd have a more grandiose way of expressing himself, but the message would be the same."

Ned seemed to pale just slightly and he appeared mortified. "Oh, man...I know how you feel about your dad. Look, just scratch everything I said, okay? I was running off at the mouth. My wife put funny ideas in my head. That's the downside of being married—they're always talking at you, and pretty soon you start thinking like them."

Craig put up his hand to make Ned stop. "I'm sure Maryanne meant well. She's a sweetheart and you're lucky to have her. But it *is* a female way of thinking—if a woman knows any bachelor over thirty, she's certain

he'd be better off married. They're all like that." Craig
had to chuckle. "Including my dad, the most conniving
'old lady' of them all."

Ned looked confused. "Your dad—an old lady?"

Craig realized he'd never mentioned his father's latest
preoccupation—matchmaking. "Well, he does needlepoint, for one thing."

Ned cracked up laughing. "You mean, like stitching
posies? You're joking."

"No. He learned it from my mother to pass the time
while he was recovering from that bad heart attack he
had a few years ago. Which was fine, but then he started
making wedding pillows."

"What's that?"

"It's like a throw pillow for a couch, and it has the
bride and groom's names and their wedding date—you
know, with lots of hearts and flowers and junk stitched
on it."

"I know what you mean—I've seen one at my great-
aunt's house."

"Remember my brother Charles? You met him when
he came here on his honeymoon?"

"Sure do."

"Charles calls it 'needlepoint voodoo.'"

"Voodoo?" Ned looked confused again.

"Dad made a pillow for them. Stitched in Charles's
name as the groom and Jennifer, my sister-in-law's name,
as the bride."

"Yeah..." Ned nodded, as if trying to understand.

"The point is, my dad made the pillow before Charles
and Jennifer even had any notion of getting married.
Maybe they knew each other because she worked at the
department store, but they weren't dating. My dad found
ways to throw them together—he even locked them in the

store overnight. Pretty soon they got married. They have a daughter now.''

"You're not making this up?" Ned asked.

"No! Then he did the same thing to my other brother, Jake. Stitched a pillow for him with the name of a girl he'd never even met. Found some way to get them to agree to a 'temporary' marriage and put them on an island in Puget Sound. I haven't met Jake's wife yet, but they've already got one kid and another on the way. Pretty soon I'll be an uncle to *three* kids!''

"And your dad made all that happen?" Ned asked incredulously.

"That's what my mom says. She's the one who writes and keeps me informed. And I'd heard Charles's story from him himself at his wedding.'' Craig paused to chuckle ominously. "So, I keep wondering when *my* turn is coming. Seems Dad's bent on marrying off all his kids before he dies. Mom wrote that it's gotten to be an obsession with him.'' He rubbed his nose self-consciously and glanced at Ned. "I guess that's why I kind of blew up at you for mentioning marriage.''

Ned smiled in an understanding way. "I get the picture. Don't worry, boss. You won't catch *me* making any needlepoint pillow!''

Both laughed heartily and the tension between them evaporated.

"So,'' Ned asked, "have you heard from your dad lately? Last time I saw him here was some years ago, before he had that heart attack.''

"No. I sent my parents a card giving them my new phone number. I kept my old Kailua-Kona P.O. box. God, if Dad found out I bought this house, he'd probably dig up some dame for me in two seconds flat! That's why, now more than ever, I've got to keep them believing that I'm just making ends meet. I need Dad to keep thinking I'm too poor to support a wife, or he'll run out and find me one. And his track record makes me nervous.''

A few weeks later Jasper was looking over a report sent by the Hawaiian private detective he'd hired, when Bea came into his office.

"Are we going out to dinner, or do you want to eat at home?" Bea asked. "It's Mabel's night off." She was referring to their cook and housekeeper.

Jasper hurriedly slid the report back into the large envelope in which it had been mailed and pushed it under some other papers. "Well, that depends on you," he said jovially. "Are you in the mood to cook?"

Bea pursed her lips. "No, not especially."

"Then we'll go out." He picked up a pen and rolled it between his fingers. "In fact, we can celebrate."

"Celebrate?"

"I . . . asked around a bit, and I have reason to believe that Craig may be somewhat more settled, financially and psychologically, than we thought."

She walked into the room and leaned her hip against Jasper's large oak desk. "How do you know?"

"Well, I've learned that Craig is not renting his new place. He's actually purchased a house."

Bea's eyes brightened. "He has? He had the money to invest in a house?"

"Apparently so."

"I'm so glad for him! Though I suppose his house is small. Probably a fixer-upper. But that's fine. He always liked to work with his hands."

Jasper knew better, but kept his knowledge to himself. He had two reasons: he knew Bea would disapprove of his investigating Craig's private life to the degree he had, and he was reluctant for her to find out from him that their son had been hiding the truth from them for so many years. He hoped Craig would eventually tell his mother himself that he was doing well.

"However small Craig's house may be," Jasper said, "it indicates a nesting instinct may have finally surfaced in him. Therefore..." He deliberately left a pregnant pause and gazed at Bea.

She eyed Jasper and straightened. "Therefore... what?" she asked, half sounding as if she didn't really want to know.

"I think it's about time Craig acquired a wife."

Bea stared up at the ceiling, as if for strength. "Jasper, you aren't going to try to play matchmaker for Craig, are you? He's not like Charles or Jake. Some men just aren't suited for marriage. Craig may very well be one of them."

Jasper pulled open the lower drawer of his desk and took out a plastic bag with the logo for Penelope's Needlepoint Shop printed on it. "I haven't shown you my latest project."

Bea looked askance. "You haven't started *another* one! Not again!"

"Oh, yes, I have," he said merrily, taking out the square canvas for the wedding pillow, stapled to a wood frame. "I've just finished figuring out how to center the names I want to stitch on it. Got the letters sketched on the canvas with my special blue ink pen. See?"

Bea covered her eyes with her hands. "No, I won't look."

"Now, Bea, you must help me on this. We both have to think positive thoughts if we're going to get Craig married off."

"I won't be a part of your needlepoint voodoo!"

"Voodoo shmoodoo," Jasper said with a laugh. "It's merely my little visualization technique. With each stitch I see Craig happily wed to…" He deliberately left the sentence unfinished, hoping Bea's curiosity would get the better of her.

Bea turned away, so she couldn't see the needlepoint canvas he was holding up in front of her. "I don't want to know what poor unsuspecting woman you've got lined up for Craig. We rarely see him, so how can you even begin to guess what would be good for him? It was different with Charles—you worked with him every day at the store. And we visited Jake in Wisconsin often enough to know him. But Craig has been so far away for so long, we don't really know who he is anymore. You can't foist a wife on your son when you don't even know what sort of woman he likes."

"Oh, I think I have a good idea," Jasper said, disregarding the logic of her argument. "Come on, take a look," he urged her, holding up the needlepoint project.

With a frustrated sigh, Bea gave in and turned her head to look. *"Penelope?"* She read the name he'd sketched on the canvas with astonishment. "The only Penelope we know is the one who runs the needlepoint shop."

"Right," Jasper said.

Bea shook her head incredulously. "Well, she's very nice, Jasper. But…she's just not the beach blanket sort!"

2

Penelope Grey stood on a metal folding chair thumb-tacking a needlepoint canvas for a Christmas stocking to the wall. She was making a display for her shop's annual "Christmas in July" sale, putting old holiday canvases on sale for half price and new ones at a special week-long twenty percent discount. She'd mailed flyers advertising the event to all her customers and had put up a sign in the window. Needlepointing was a time-consuming hobby, and midsummer was when most customers would need to start their Christmas projects to have them done by December.

"Ouch!" she exclaimed. The thumbtack in her fingers had turned unexpectedly and scraped her thumb. Fortunately the scrape wasn't deep enough to bleed, but annoying enough to make her exasperated and anxious to get the display finished.

Penelope wasn't in the best of moods today, feeling vaguely out-of-sorts, and dealing with holiday merchandise only reminded her of how she always got depressed at Thanksgiving and Christmas. Like many people, she didn't have any large family gatherings to look forward to at that time of year.

As she hung the last Christmas canvas, a tired sigh puffed out her cheeks. Carefully, she got down from the chair and slid it back under the long table she used when conducting her weekly needlepoint class.

A car pulling up in front of her shop caught her eye and she glanced out the window. She recognized the black Mercedes-Benz sedan. It belonged to one of her best customers, Jasper Derring. She always felt honored—and a bit floored—to have the famous department store baron shopping in *her* little store. But he was so friendly, if a tad eccentric, that she always felt at home with him.

She watched as he got out of the car. Jasper was surprisingly short in height, considering his power and status in Chicago, but his brown-black eyes always sparkled with energy and quick perception beneath his bushy gray eyebrows. His hair was a stately gray-white, and he usually wore fine-quality clothes. It was the first of July, and he was suitably dressed in tan pants and a white-and-tan striped shirt.

He generally came by in the afternoon, so she was surprised to see him so early in the morning. She watched as he walked to the other side of the car and opened the door for his wife, Bea. A slim, delicate woman, Bea was the same height as her husband. Penelope smiled as she realized Bea was wearing her hair tied back the same way that she was. They both were also wearing long, flowered, broomstick skirts. It amused Penelope to know she liked the same style as a millionaire's wife.

Bea had actually been her customer first, but then Jasper had started coming in, too, a few years ago. Jasper sometimes stopped in by himself, usually shopping for commemorative wedding canvases.

Penelope eagerly walked to the glass door to open it for them.

* * *

As Jasper shut the door of his car, his heart beating with the anticipation of putting his new plan into effect, Bea whispered, "Are you really going to go through with this?"

"Of course," Jasper said.

"I sense disaster."

"*Non*sense," he told his wife. "Shoo those negative thoughts out of your mind!"

"I'm too practical for positive thinking," Bea said. "I know I can't stop you from setting up poor Penelope, but why do I have to be along for the kill?"

"She likes you," Jasper explained. "She'll feel more comfortable accepting my offer if you're there when I put it to her. And you'll be able to describe Craig in more glowing terms than I could ever come up with." He glanced at the door and saw Penelope opening it for them. "There she is," he whispered to Bea. "Just follow my lead. Think happy thoughts! We're doing the right thing."

Bea squinted at him. "Oh, you can promise me that absolutely?"

"Shh!" He tugged Bea by the hand and walked to the open door where Penelope was smiling at them. "Morning!" he greeted the young woman.

"Hi, Jasper," Penelope replied. "You're bright and early! Hello, Bea." She shook their hands. "Come to see what I've got for the Christmas in July sale?"

"Sure. We've got another grandchild on the way," Jasper said with pride. "Need another Christmas stocking for the fireplace. Bea came to help me pick one out."

Bea smiled, but her gaze drifted to the tiled floor.

"Well, there are some on display on the wall," Penelope told them, pointing, "and lots more on hangers on the rack."

"I'll start looking," Bea said, as if anxious to be doing something.

"How's business?" Jasper asked.

"Pretty good," Penelope replied. "I think I may manage to put aside enough money to visit my mother in Florida for a few days at Christmas again this year."

"That's nice. She'll appreciate it, I'm sure. But what about a vacation this summer?" Jasper noticed signs of weariness in her eyes. Her cheeks looked slightly gaunt, as if from fatigue.

Penelope was a slim, pretty young woman, though some might overlook her because she dressed simply and didn't adorn herself with makeup or jewelry. Usually she wore her thick brown hair loose and flowing over her shoulders, but today she had it tied back with a ribbon—probably to keep cool in the summer heat. To Jasper, she always seemed modest and unassuming, but he intuited that she had a definite sense of herself. Penelope was genuine—a rare quality nowadays. She reminded Jasper of Bea when he first met her years and years ago.

Jasper realized she was chuckling at his question, and it quickly brought him back to the present. He got his mind in gear. "Why do you smile?" he asked.

"I haven't had a vacation in six years, not since I opened this place. I've never felt I could afford to close the shop for any length of time."

"You look a little tired," Jasper said in a gentle tone. "Maybe you need one. You're open six days a week. I imagine you must be overworked. You probably could do with a change of scene."

"I suppose I could. But since I'm visiting my mom in December, I don't have enough money for any other out-of-town trip. Airfare and hotels are expensive. If I'm going to stay in Chicago, I'd just as soon go to work."

Jasper studied her and stroked his chin. "If you could travel anywhere in the world, where would you like to go?"

Penelope lifted her shoulders in a graceful shrug. "Gosh, I don't know. Maybe Norway. I'd like to see the fjords."

"Mmm. What about Hawaii?"

"Hawaii? Well, sure, that would be nice, too. I've never been there. I've never been anywhere. My parents didn't have the money to travel."

"I own a condo on the Kona coast on the Big Island. It's near the town of Kailua-Kona. I bought it years ago. I thought Bea and I might use it for vacations, but she's always been reluctant."

Bea turned from the Christmas stocking canvases she was perusing. "I have trouble with motion sickness," she explained. "Don't like to fly."

Penelope nodded, as if in accord. "I know. I tend to have trouble with that, too."

Oh, terrific, Jasper dourly thought to himself, wishing Bea hadn't brought up her problems and put Penelope off the idea of flying anywhere.

"But you know what I discovered?" Penelope went on, talking to Bea across the room. "Last year at Christmas, my mother told me about a friend who uses wristbands for motion sickness. So I bought some at the drugstore. I wore them on a boat excursion with my mom, and I was just fine. On the plane home, too. I was amazed how well it worked."

Jasper's eyes widened. "Really?" he said with renewed energy.

Bea walked up to the front counter where Penelope and Jasper were standing. She held a couple of canvases in her hands. "Wristbands?" she asked Penelope. "How do they work?"

"They're elastic, and they have two round knobs sewn in that you have to place just at the right spots on the inside of your wrists. They keep you from getting nauseous. It's like accupressure."

"I've never heard of that," Bea said, looking astonished.

"Me, either," Penelope told her. "I think it's sort of new. But it worked great."

"I'll have to get some and have Jasper take me on a long, bumpy car ride. See if it works for me, too!"

Jasper eagerly rubbed his hands together. "We'll stop at a drugstore on the way home." Maybe he could actually get Bea to fly to Hawaii with him to observe his plan in operation. Of course, she'd be chiding him the whole time, but he'd still rather have her along.

"So, about Hawaii," he said, bringing the subject back to where he'd left off, "I'd be happy to let you stay in my condo, rent-free, Penelope."

Penelope looked startled, her blue eyes widening. "Oh, I couldn't do that—"

"Why not?"

"Well—"

"You've done so much—teaching me all about needlepoint, helping me choose yarns and colors, showing me ornate stitches—and this would be a nice way for me to repay you."

"But, Jasper, I do that for all my customers," Penelope said. "It's part of my job."

"Yes, but I'm in here more than most of your clientele, asking questions, taking up your time. And the offer I'm making you costs me nothing. The condo's there, standing empty. Someone might as well use it. Why not you?"

Penelope looked down and shook her head. "Even if I felt I could accept your offer, there's still the airfare. It's expensive to fly from Chicago to Hawaii."

"I have a lot of accumulated frequent flier mileage that I won't be able to use up before it expires. I can get you free tickets." Jasper spread his hands outward, palms up. "Won't cost me a dime."

Penelope still appeared troubled and she looked at Bea, as if to ask silently, *Do you think this is all right?*

Now's the time, Bea, Jasper thought, trying some mental telepathy to get his reluctant wife to respond as he wished.

Bea hesitated, and Jasper nervously twitched his nose. Then she said to Penelope with her characteristic truthfulness, "You do look tired, dear. A vacation anywhere would be good for you."

Jasper breathed easier and chimed in, "Hawaii's the most restful place in the world. Nice weather, palm trees swaying in the ocean breezes, the sound of the waves— my condo's in a choice location to soak in the atmosphere and relax. You'll enjoy it. Come back totally refreshed!"

Penelope smiled. "I appreciate the offer, but...I'd need to think about it."

"No, don't think!" Jasper said jovially, shaking his finger at her. "Make a spur of the moment decision! Those are the best kind."

She laughed as if discombobulated. "When would I go?"

"Before this month is over," Jasper advised. "August is the busiest time for tourism there, so you'd do well to avoid the crowds. How about next week?"

"So soon?"

"The week after, then."

Penelope grinned, rubbed her pale cheek, and gazed at Bea. "You're married to an impetuous man!"

Bea nodded, raising her eyebrows in a resigned yet humorous expression. "You have no idea how impetuous." She smiled almost sympathetically. "You know you might as well say yes, because once Jasper gets an idea in his head, he's relentless."

"Say yes, say yes!" Jasper urged.

Penelope sighed. "I am tired," she admitted. "If you're sure you want to do this, I'd be thrilled to go. It sounds wonderful."

"Great!" Jasper said with secret relief.

"But what'll I do about the store?" A fretful expression came over Penelope's face.

"Put a Closed sign in the window," Jasper suggested.

"Yes, I guess that's what I'll have to do." She seemed to be thinking it through as she spoke. "I suppose it won't hurt to close the place for a week."

"Make it two weeks," Jasper quickly advised.

"Two? Oh, no, I'd lose too much revenue. My customers might find some other needlepoint store to go to if I'm closed for that long."

"Now, now," Jasper said, reaching out to pat her hand. "I wouldn't buy my needlepoint supplies anywhere but here, and I'm sure none of your other customers would either. And when you come back all relaxed and renewed, you'll be able to operate your business at an optimum level. Take advice from a successful businessman," he said, pointing to his chest. "In the long run, fatigue is more harmful than the temporary loss of a few revenue dollars.''

Penelope looked suitably overwhelmed. Jasper knew she'd have a hard time arguing business with a self-made millionaire.

"If you say so," she said, lifting her shoulders. "I suppose the famous Jasper Derring ought to know."

"You bet!"

She studied Jasper with worried eyes. "I don't know how I can ever repay the favor."

"I told you," he assured her, "you've already repayed me by teaching me a hobby that's meant a lot to me. My recuperation from my heart attack was difficult, and needlepointing helped me through it. Now I'm enjoying my semiretirement with a pastime I love, and the reason is you've taught me so much to make it enjoyable. Believe me, *I'm* indebted to *you*." He paused. Out of the corner of his eye, he could see Bea eyeing him suspiciously. He continued nevertheless. "Though—now that I think of it—there is one little thing you could do for me while you're there in Kailua...that is if you don't mind," he told Penelope.

"Of course," the young woman replied, looking grateful. "Anything."

"Our eldest son lives there. Craig. I think I may have mentioned him."

Penelope's expression changed slightly. "Yes. He...he left years ago and became sort of a beachcomber?"

"Yes, that's the one—handsomest fellow in the whole Derring family, but has trouble finding the ambition to make anything of himself. Such a shame." Jasper clicked his tongue to show his disappointment. "Perhaps you could look him up, see how he's doing? Bea worries about him, as you might imagine. Mothers always worry.

And so do I. He takes tourists out on snorkeling excursions. That's how he makes what living he has. Owns an old boat in the bay there.''

"Oh." Penelope's forehead creased. "How would I check up on him? What would I say?"

"Perhaps you could just hire him to take you out snorkeling. God knows, he probably could use the business. Maybe you can get him to talk about himself, and then you can let us know if he seems to be doing all right. I've often offered to send money, but he's always refused to take anything more than what we gave him as a graduation present years ago. And he squandered that in no time."

Penelope had begun chewing on her fingernail. "I'd like to, Jasper, but I don't swim. Snorkeling isn't something I'd do. I'm sorry, but—"

"Hire him to take you on a tour of the Kona coast, then."

"Jasper," Bea said, "maybe she's like me and doesn't like boats."

"Actually, I don't," Penelope said.

"But you have those wristbands now, so you won't get seasick. You went on that boat with your mother in Florida, didn't you?"

"Yes, but that was because *she* wanted to." Penelope paused, then made a little shrug, as if reminding herself of the free vacation Jasper was bestowing on her. "Well, sure, I can hire him for a boat ride. A short one. I can... take him out to lunch, too."

"Excellent. More than kind," Jasper said.

"Should I tell him I know you?" she asked, looking unsure of her assignment.

"That's up to you," Jasper replied.

"Okay. So...you just want me to see if he looks healthy?"

"Yes, and perhaps get him talking. Ask him how business is, that sort of thing."

Penelope nodded. "Sure, okay. I'll...be happy to." She tried to smile. But Jasper noticed she still looked a little worried and he wondered why.

"He's a fine young man," Bea told her, apparently better at interpreting Penelope's uneasy expression than he was. "Jasper tends to paint an unflattering picture of our son because he disapproves of his chosen life. But Craig isn't the sort who would take advantage of you in any way. You don't have to worry about being out on a boat with him. He's trustworthy. He just likes a simpler life-style than he was born to. Jasper always hopes he'll change, but I'm happy for Craig as long as he's happy." Bea's eyebrows drew together in an earnest expression. "Though I do wonder if he's eating properly and taking care of himself," she added with a sigh.

Jasper smiled smugly and knew he need not add anything to Bea's statements regarding their footloose son. He was glad he'd managed to talk her into coming along. Women always seemed to communicate well with one another.

Penelope seemed satisfied with Bea's reassurance. "All right," she said agreeably, "I'll look him up."

Jasper decided it was exactly the right time to make an exit, before Penelope could rethink her decision. "Found a Christmas stocking you like?" he asked Bea, looking at the two canvases she still held in her hands.

"I like both of these," Bea said. "You decide, since you'll be stitching it." She held them up for him to see.

One had an old-fashioned Santa Claus on it and the other a colorful Christmas tree. "They're equally appealing,'' he told her. ''Can't decide. Let's take them both.''

Penelope smiled. ''But you have only one new grandchild on the way, don't you? Or is your daughter-in-law expecting twins?''

''No, she's had ultrasound and there's only one on the way,'' Bea said with amusement. ''But I imagine Jasper is assuming there'll be yet another grandchild, sooner or later.'' She turned to Jasper.

Jasper said nothing and hoped his smile wasn't too much like a Cheshire cat's.

After Jasper and Bea had left with their canvases, Penelope had to sit down on the folding chair, reeling a bit, wondering how she could have made such an impulsive decision. She couldn't imagine how Jasper could be so generous. It wasn't as if she was a relative of his, or even a close friend. But then, he was a millionaire, and perhaps he liked to do philanthropic favors for people he knew and liked.

Still, she felt guilty somehow for accepting such a generous offer. What had she done to deserve it? She really hadn't helped Jasper with his needlepoint all that much. Actually Bea had taught him the two basic stitches, the continental and the basketweave. Penelope had only helped him choose colors and demonstrated how to center the lettering on his pieces. She'd also shown him a couple of different background stitches he hadn't known. But as she'd told him, she'd done the same for many of her customers.

Despite her feelings of guilt, however, she *was* tired. She had the feeling her life was in a rut, and good luck seldom came her way. Why refuse a piece of good luck when it did fall into her lap? Last year, a friend of hers had won a European vacation in a contest she'd entered. Penelope had envied her. Now she'd gotten a free vacation of her own—not through a contest, but through the benevolence of a favorite customer. Was it so different? Oh, stop worrying about it and just go! she told herself.

She wasn't thrilled, however, about having to look up Jasper's son. Jasper had talked about Craig the last time he'd come in, a couple of weeks ago. He'd said enough about Craig that day to make Penelope disinclined to meet him.

Craig sounded very similar to Penelope's ne'er-do-well father, who was handsome and charming as a man could be, but could never hold down a job for more than six months. He'd always gotten restless, wouldn't show up for work, and eventually got fired. Then he'd talk his way into another job, only to have the same pattern play out again.

It was her mother who had kept their small family together—until he left it to run off with a wealthy divorcée when Penelope was a teenager. Penelope hadn't see him again until seven years ago, just before he died, in debt and alone.

After he died, her mother had moved to Florida for its warmer climate with money she'd inherited when her mother, Penelope's grandmother, passed away about six years ago. She'd inherited enough to help Penelope set herself up in her needlepoint shop.

Her mother, thank goodness, was finally living a contented life in Florida on her own. Several retired widowers courted her, but her mother had vowed never to marry again. Penelope didn't blame her. Sometimes she wondered if she shouldn't stay single herself. Still, she always had a secret wish to be married—happily married, if there was such a thing.

Life with her father had been precarious, though she did have bittersweet memories of him telling her she was the prettiest little girl in the world. But sweet talk was all he had to offer and there was never any money for clothes for school or for Christmas and birthday presents. Because of her early disillusionment with the most important man in her life, Penelope avoided dating men who struck her as irresponsible. She wanted to be more sensible than her mother had been. In fact, her mother always cautioned her not to make the same mistake.

Unfortunately, the prospective males Penelope met who were reliable and responsible never seemed to appeal to her. Like her mother, she was most attracted to men who were charming and devil-may-care. Steady-Eddy types just didn't seem to sweep her off her feet the way she imagined the man of her dreams should. She was almost twenty-nine. In another year she'd be pushing thirty. At her age, if she really expected to marry anyone, she should give up on the idea of meeting a "dream man." With her life experience, she ought to know better, she often chided herself.

But the silent wish in her heart didn't seem to die, and Penelope feared that her common sense vying with her romantic demands would keep her an old maid forever. She could see her life, centered around her shop, becoming more and more circumscribed, more and more uneventful.

Yes, she needed a vacation. Hawaii was just what the doctor ordered. Having to see Craig Derring would only be a minor inconvenience. One brief boat ride with a beach bum was a small trade-off for what promised to be a marvelous holiday.

3

Two weeks later Penelope flew to Oahu. After landing in Honolulu, she caught an inter-island flight to Keahole Airport, located on the western, leeward side of the Big Island, Hawaii. There she got the rental car, a small convertible, that Jasper had reserved for her. She drove south along the Kona coast toward Kailua-Kona, surprised at the flatness of the landscape and the outcroppings of rough black rock. But when she reached the town of Kailua-Kona, it looked picturesque and busy with tourists wandering happily from shop to shop. She found Alii Drive and continued south, following Jasper's directions. The landscape became more green and lush, more like she had pictured Hawaii would be. Inland, there were hills. Eventually she found the modern, oceanfront villa that was her destination.

She parked in the numbered spot that matched the apartment number, as Jasper had told her to. The condo was on the top floor, so she took an elevator up and used the key Jasper had given her to let herself in. The condo was stuffy and rather dark because the draperies were drawn. She walked past upholstered chairs and a sofa to the floor-to-ceiling draperies and opened them. A breathtaking view of the ocean, with waves lapping onto a rocky beach, met her eyes. The sun was shining and a

line of palm trees shifted in the breeze. She unlocked and
opened the sliding-glass doors, breathed in the glori-
ously fresh air and walked out onto the balcony. A small
table and two deck chairs sat as if waiting to be used,
along with a recliner for sunbathing. Penelope smiled to
herself, thinking she could happily spend her whole two-
week vacation right here, enjoying the sun while catching up on her reading, gazing out at the peaceful ocean
whenever she felt like it.

Eventually she went back in and explored the comfortable living room, the bedroom with its queen-size
bed, and the kitchen. She'd seen a small grocery store
near the building's entrance, so she went down and
bought herself some snack foods, breakfast cereal, bread,
juice, eggs, and milk. Late in the afternoon, she drove
into town, shopped a bit, found a cozy little restaurant to
have dinner, and then drove back. It was only eight
o'clock local time, but her body was still on Chicago
time, and in Chicago it was 1:00 a.m. She finished unpacking, put on her shorty nightgown and went to bed.
Relaxed already, she soon fell soundly asleep.

Craig sat behind the wheel of his Porsche sports car,
reluctantly driving to his father's condo. He'd decided he
might as well go there; it was better than staying at a hotel filled with tourists. Craig had to deal with tourists all
day. Ned had invited him to stay at his house, but Craig
didn't want to intrude on his family. Years ago, Jasper
had given him the key to his condo, telling him he was
always welcome to stay there if he needed a place. Craig
suspected Jasper had bought the condo just for that
purpose shortly after Craig had settled near Kailua-Kona.
Craig didn't want the key, told his dad he could take care
of himself, but Jasper had insisted. Tonight was the first

time Craig had ever had a need to stay there. He didn't plan to tell his dad.

Ned had finished work on the yacht, so Craig had bitten the bullet and told him to go ahead and begin refinishing the wood floors of his home. His friend had been right—he couldn't keep putting it off.

Craig had spent the morning helping Ned move the few pieces of furniture he had in the bedroom and other rooms, and tossing out old items left by the previous owner. Then he'd gone to his office. After working late going over tour schedules, he'd stopped home briefly to pick up some clothes and his toothbrush. Ned had already left for the day. He found his magnificent home filled with dust, because Ned had been sanding down the old wood floors. It was a good thing the place was still mostly unfurnished, Craig had thought to himself, fingering the thick dust that had settled on the kitchen counters.

He'd forgotten to eat dinner, so he'd grabbed some crackers out of his kitchen and some leftover cheese spread from the fridge. After snacking on that, he'd found the key to his dad's condo in a drawer, left Ned a note that he'd stop by in the morning, and gotten in his car.

While on the road, he noticed a white car in his rearview mirror that, oddly, seemed to be following him. Craig's car was brand new and the situation made him nervous, so he took a few quick turns down back roads and lost the white car.

When Craig finally pulled in to his dad's place, he was annoyed to find a convertible in Jasper's parking spot. Someone must not have realized the parking places were reserved. He found a different spot, parked, and took the elevator to the top floor. When he entered the condo, he was a little surprised to find the draperies open. People usually left them closed to keep out the sun's heat and bleaching rays. The full moon hanging over the ocean lit the place well enough to see, so Craig didn't bother turning on the lights. After glancing over the living room and small kitchen, he noted that the place hadn't changed much since Jasper bought it. Years ago Jasper had asked him to look it over before he invested in it, and that was the last time Craig had seen the place.

The door to the bedroom was ajar, but Craig didn't go in. Instead, he set his duffel bag on the living room couch, opened the sliding-glass doors and walked outside. As usual, it was a beautiful night. The breeze felt cool and refreshing. He took a gander at the lounge chair and decided it looked comfortable. Rather than mess up the clean linens on the bed, Craig decided he'd just sleep out here on the lanai. He liked to fall asleep to the sound of the waves anyway. It was almost like home. Almost. He hoped Ned could finish his floors as fast as he'd finished the boat.

Still on Chicago time, Penelope woke up at dawn. Unable to fall back to sleep, she decided she might as well get up. She stretched in her rose-print cotton nightgown and walked out of the bedroom into the living room. She was surprised to see the sliding doors wide open—she thought for sure she'd closed and locked them before going to bed. Safety had always been important to her, and she never forgot to lock a door at night.

She grew a little scared. Had someone gotten in? But the condo was on the fourth floor, and it would have been difficult for anyone to get in from the balcony. Holding her breath, she tiptoed barefoot toward the open doors. She saw the small table and two chairs set just as they had been last night. Pausing at the edge, where the sliding door met the pulled-back drapery, she peeked around it— and screamed.

A man lay sound asleep on the lounge chair. At her scream, he jerked upright and toppled over, along with the chair, long legs and arms flying.

"Help!" she exclaimed. "Help!" She ran into the kitchen. On the counter next to the stove stood a small-size fire extinguisher. She grabbed it, hurried back to the doorway and pointed the nozzle at him.

He was still getting up off the tiled floor.

"What are you doing here?" she demanded, pointing the nozzle as menacingly as she could. She was all too conscious of the fact that she'd never used a fire extinguisher in her life and wasn't sure how to turn it on if she needed to.

"S-sleeping," he said, his green eyes wide, his speech thick. He looked groggy, as though he was desperately trying to get his bearings. His half-awake manner made him seem rather harmless, but when he straightened to his full height, Penelope's terror was renewed. He stood over six feet tall, and appeared to be in magnificent physical shape. He made a handsome intruder, with his ruffled brown hair that looked sun-bleached on top, a straight, narrow nose and sensual mouth. But he looked as if he hadn't shaved for a couple of days and he wore a faded T-shirt and cutoffs that had a few holes in them. He wet his lips as if his mouth was dry and asked, "Who are you?"

"Who are *you?*" she countered, still pointing the red fire extinguisher at him.

"Craig Derring. My dad owns this place."

"Oh." *Jasper's son,* she thought to herself. *The beach bum.* "You're staying here?" she asked.

"Just for a few nights."

Probably has nowhere else to go, Penelope thought. "Does Jasper know?"

"You know my dad?" Craig asked, raising his eyebrows.

"Yes. He's letting *me* stay here for two weeks for my vacation."

Craig nodded his head, as if beginning to put things together in his mind. "I see."

"Jasper never mentioned that you used this place. Have you been living here?"

"No," he said, sounding a little annoyed. "I've never stayed here before. It's just that, at the moment, I can't go home."

Maybe he was living with a girlfriend and she threw him out, Penelope thought. She could see how that might happen. He was certainly handsome enough to attract a woman, but he'd probably mooched on her until she'd tossed him out. Just like Penelope's father and the divorcée he'd run off with.

"Well," she said, raising her chin. "Then that creates a problem, since your father has promised this place to me."

He drew a long breath and rubbed his eye. She noticed he wore an elaborate-looking black watch, one that not only told digital time but also had other gadgets and was probably waterproof, too. The obviously expensive watch looked incongruous with the rest of his clothes. Perhaps an old gift from the girlfriend, Penelope decided.

"That's fine," he said. "I'll go somewhere else." He took his hand from his face and gazed at her with amusement in his sleepy eyes. "You can put down that extinguisher. I'm not going to set anything on fire."

I wonder, Penelope thought ominously as she gazed at him, her senses still oddly heightened though she no longer felt in danger. She began to realize she might be vulnerable to a different sort of danger. If he kept on looking at her with those bedroom eyes, he was liable to set *her* on fire. She quickly glanced down to hide her unexpected reaction. Lowering the nozzle, she turned and set the extinguisher on the small table between the two chairs. The sooner this guy left, the better, she told herself.

When she turned around, she found him looking her over, especially her bare legs showing beneath her mid-thigh-length nightgown. She quickly pulled down on the nightgown, as if trying to stretch it. Despite her efforts at modesty, he still stared at her, taking her in from head to toe. He certainly wasn't shy. Perhaps in that way he took after Jasper.

"What's your name?" he asked.

"Penelope Grey."

His mouth formed a quirky smile. "Penelope. Don't run into that name too often. It's from Greek mythology, right? Odysseus's wife?"

"So I've heard," she replied.

"How do you know my dad?"

"He and Bea come to my shop quite often."

"Shop?" His eyes glinted with amiable curiosity.

"I own a needlepoint shop," she explained.

At that, the lights in his gaze disappeared and his eyes refocused on her in a wary, almost cold manner. "Needlepoint," he repeated, nodding his head as if he were reading much more into her answer than she ever meant. "Now I see why he sent you here." His tone was beginning to sound bitter.

"Sent me? I don't understand . . ."

He sniffed, twitching his handsome nose. His expression softened. "No, you probably don't." He gazed at her with kinder eyes. "Never mind. It's a...family joke, that's all."

"Something about needlepoint?"

"Yeah. I guess you don't know my dad all that well. He's just a good customer?"

"Yes. And a very generous one. When I told him I couldn't afford a vacation, he offered to let me stay here free."

"He can be generous," Craig readily agreed. "I bet he covered your airfare, too."

She nodded. "He said he had frequent flier mileage that he couldn't use himself."

Craig smiled in a knowing way. "And how was it that you were telling him you couldn't afford a vacation? Just small talk?"

Penelope was puzzled by his questions. It was as if he was suspicious or something. "Yes," she said, feeling self-conscious now for accepting Jasper's offer, since his son seemed to be doubting the situation. "He mentioned that I looked tired and asked me if I was going to take a vacation."

"Aha," Craig said quietly, looking even more amused. "And you said you couldn't afford one, and Jasper told you about this place and made you a wonderful offer you couldn't refuse. Or did he even give you a chance to refuse?"

She chuckled uneasily. "He was persistent, all right."

"That's my dad, for you. And my mom? Was she there?"

"Yes. She agreed that I looked tired and a vacation would do me good."

"Hmm," Craig said, turning to look out at the brightening morning sky. He glanced back at Penelope, his demeanor more resolved. "Okay. I'll go and let you have the place to yourself. Sorry I scared you. I had no idea my dad had given the place to anyone, or I wouldn't have come here at all."

He walked into the living room and picked up a duffel bag she hadn't noticed before. Suddenly, Penelope felt guilt-stricken for more or less chasing him out. She remembered how worried Jasper and Bea were about him. The one favor Jasper had asked was that she check up on Craig.

"Is there somewhere you can go?" she asked as he swung the bag over his shoulder.

"Sure. I've got friends on the island I can stay with."

"I feel badly now, putting you out. Actually, Jasper asked me to look you up."

Craig studied her with a certain perverse merriment in his eyes. "Did he?"

"He, um, recommended you as a good person to take me snorkeling."

Craig blinked. "I do have a catamaran." He looked her up and down again. "*You* want to go snorkeling?"

Penelope bit her lip. He seemed to have guessed that she wasn't the outdoors type. Her pale skin always gave her away. "Well, I'm not exactly a water person," she admitted. "A scenic tour of the coastline would be better."

He smiled and shook his head ever so slightly. "Not a 'water' person? You don't swim?"

"I learned in high school. But I don't especially like to swim. I've never done it much, even when I was a teenager. I didn't live near a pool and taking public transportation all the way to Lake Michigan was a lot of trouble.''

"City girl, eh?''

"Yes.''

"I grew up in Chicago, too,'' he said. "I was out of my element there. This is where I was meant to be.''

"I'm . . . glad you're happy.'' She looked down at his worn clothes. "Can you make a good living here, though?''

He shifted his eyes. "Good enough. Always lots of tourists coming here. Most of them want to go snorkeling—except for a few, like you.''

She felt he was giving her a mild put-down and it piqued her slightly. "I just don't like to get wet.''

He laughed, making the corners of his eyes crinkle. "Why?''

"The water stings my nose and eyes. Plugs up my ears. My hair gets wet, and then I have to dry it. And then there's smearing on all that messy sunscreen. I never thought swimming was worth it.''

He shook his forefinger at her. "You really ought to go snorkeling. You don't know what you're missing.''

"A few fish swimming around?''

He glanced upward as if he'd never heard such a comment before. "Spectacular fish in so many varieties you lose count. Schools of them. And the coral canyons they swim through are silent and beautiful. It's a tranquil, amazing world under the sea.''

"Yes, well . . . it's pretty above the water, too.''

"I can see you're a challenge.'' He gave her a keen look. "When would you like to go?''

"On your boat?''

"Catamaran. Yes.''

"Oh . . . whenever you have time.''

"This afternoon?" he suggested. "I can make time."

That was much too soon for Penelope. She knew she wanted to get her obligation to Jasper out of the way as soon as possible, but she needed to get used to the idea, too. "How about tomorrow?"

"Okay. Morning or afternoon?"

"Afternoon?" she said, her voice weakening.

"Fine," he said. "Got a suit?"

"Bathing suit?"

"Yes."

"Sure, I brought one. Do I need it for just a boat ride?"

"You should take it along in case you change your mind about snorkeling."

She wasn't anxious to be seen in her suit, especially around him. The way he kept eyeing her made her nervous. It also made her excited, and that worried her. He was exactly the type of man she'd vowed to stay away from.

On the other hand, she probably needn't worry too much about attracting him. Her bathing suit wasn't exactly up-to-date. And her figure wasn't exactly like Christie Brinkley's. Penelope was a little on the lean side, and he looked like a man who appreciated a well-filled bikini. She was safe, even if he talked her into putting on her suit.

"Tomorrow, then," he said. "Be ready at two."

He began to leave and she found herself asking, "Would you like some breakfast?"

He turned, looking surprised. "You don't have to offer me breakfast."

"I know, but I feel bad for waking you up in such a rude manner," she said with a smile. "Especially since your dad has been so kind to me. The least I can do is

offer you some cereal, or toast and eggs." Penelope was
thinking of Bea, knowing she wouldn't want her son sent
away on an empty stomach.

He stared at her a long moment. "Toast and eggs?" he
repeated as if tempted. "Orange juice, too?"

"I bought grapefruit juice."

"Figures. Okay, I'm hungry enough to take you up on
that offer. I never got around to eating dinner last night."

Too broke to eat, Penelope surmised. She felt a little
sorry for him. He *was* a personable fellow. He seemed to
be just as Jasper had described, the handsomest one of
his family, but unable to make anything of himself. Why
did it always turn out that way with these appealing ne'er-
do-wells? Penelope warned herself not to start feeling too
sorry for him.

She grew conscious that she was still dressed in her
brief nightgown. "Wait a second while I put on some
clothes, and then I'll cook breakfast."

He nodded and set his duffel bag back on the couch.
As she walked into the bedroom, she had the strong feeling that his eyes were on her, but she didn't dare turn to
verify her suspicion. It might look as if she were flirting,
and she wanted to be sure not to send any signals he could
misread.

Craig chuckled silently as the bedroom door closed. So
this was the woman dear old dad had selected for *him*.
Well, Jasper must have lost his touch, because Penelope
was exactly the sort of overdelicate, prissy type he'd decided by age twenty he'd never be attracted to. God, she
was even afraid to put her toe in the ocean! How could
Jasper think that she'd be a match for him? Pale, unad-
venturous, full of propriety—these were qualities Craig
never looked for in a female. Great legs, though. Nice

hair, too, though there seemed to be too much of it for her frail frame. And she was gracious, offering him breakfast even after he'd half scared her to death. He'd never forget the image of her in her little baby-doll nightie pointing the fire extinguisher at him.

No, he couldn't blame her for the situation his dad had put them in. She probably had no idea she was being set up as bait in Jasper's marriage trap. But how could Jasper have known that Craig would decide to use this condo, so he could maneuver Penelope into staying here at just the right time? Actually, Jasper couldn't have known, because Craig had only decided last night to stay here, and he hadn't told anyone. And Penelope must have already been here when he made the decision.

Maybe it was just one of those weird coincidences. Penelope did say that Jasper had asked her to look him up for a snorkeling tour. That was probably the way he'd planned for them to meet. How odd that they met this way. Craig was reminded of Jasper's "needlepoint voodoo." Was the voodoo at work already?

Craig shuddered and told himself he was being stupid. He didn't believe in voodoo or telepathy or synchronicity, or any of that Twilight Zone stuff. They'd met by accident, and that's all there was to it.

Restless now, he got up and decided to see if there was some coffee around that he could start making while he waited for Penelope. He found some small vacuum-packed coffee bags she'd set at the back of the counter. They were samples of different flavors. He picked Kona Roast and turned on the faucet to fill the glass server from the small coffee maker.

He was just turning on the machine to brew when she came in, dressed in bermuda shorts and a new-looking yellow T-shirt with bright tropical flowers and the word Hawaii printed on it.

"Been shopping?" he asked, eyeing the shirt.

She smiled. "I went into town for a little while after I arrived yesterday."

"You flew in only yesterday?"

"Yes."

God, their both coming to Jasper's condo for the first time on the same day *was* a huge coincidence.

"How do you like your eggs?" she asked.

"Scrambled."

"That's easy," she said, taking four eggs out of the refrigerator. She took out butter and a loaf of bread. "Would you make the toast?"

"Be glad to," he replied. He opened the cellophane covering the bread. "So, what do you plan to do while you're here?"

She broke an egg into a bowl. "Just relax. Read. Do some needlework."

"Sounds nice, but I bet you'll get tired of that after a couple of days. You should take a helicopter ride over the volcanoes. Kilauea is active, you know. The helicopter will take you right over the lava flows. It's pretty spectacular."

Penelope shook her head as she broke the last egg into the bowl. "I don't even like airplanes. There's no way I'm getting in a helicopter, especially one that goes over an erupting volcano!"

"Okay," he said. Maybe that was a little too adventurous for someone like her. "There's a submarine tour you can take. It goes down about a hundred feet to the ocean floor. It would be a good way to see the fish and coral, since you don't want to snorkel."

She sighed as she beat the eggs with a fork. "I'd get claustrophobic."

"I see," he said, searching his brain for another suggestion. "Then how about whale watching? There's a nice three-and-a-half hour tour that takes you to see the whales and dolphins. They provide binoculars and everything."

"Three and a half hours? That's kind of a long time to be stuck on a boat. I had to spend several hours on a plane to get here."

"Right." Craig was running out of ideas. "I guess scuba diving is out. Deep-sea fishing?"

Penelope merely laughed as she poured the beaten eggs into a hot frying pan.

"Parasailing?"

"What's that?" she asked.

"They hitch you up to a parachute and pull you along behind a motorboat."

She shook her head. "Why would anybody want to do something like that? Have you?"

"Sure."

"You liked it?"

"Not as much as sailing and snorkeling, but it was fun."

"Good grief," she muttered as she stirred the eggs in the pan.

"There are some excellent golf courses here. Do you play golf?"

"Just once. I thought it was boring."

Craig wondered how she could distinguish between golf and the rest of her life, but refrained from making the comment aloud.

"The eggs are almost done," she told him. "Better put the bread in the toaster."

Craig quickly set about doing the task he'd forgotten. He found dishes in the cupboard and set the table. As she portioned out the scrambled eggs, he poured the grapefruit juice. They sat down to eat.

The simple breakfast tasted delicious to Craig, who hadn't had a decent meal since lunch yesterday. He forked down his food with gusto. When he looked up, he found Penelope watching him.

"You *are* hungry!" she said with a smile. He noted that it was rather a sad smile, as if she felt sympathy for him. Or sorry for him. He realized that she might be assuming he was too poor to buy food. Earlier, when he'd explained he couldn't go home, he'd seen the same expression on her face, especially as she'd eyed his clothing. He'd put on old clothes yesterday because he'd needed to help Ned move furniture. He hadn't bothered to change because he'd stayed holed up in his office the rest of the day with paperwork. No use dressing all crisp and new if he wasn't going to be dealing personally with tourists.

Craig had the urge to tell her he wasn't homeless, but then he remembered that she was Jasper's friend. He didn't want it getting back to his dad that he even owned a home, much less could afford to have it remodeled, so he let Penelope assume what she wanted. Jasper may have even told her he lived a beachcomber's life—though he couldn't see why his dad would do that if he was secretly presenting him as husband material to Penelope.

"Are you sure you can find a place to stay tonight?" she asked, looking troubled now.

He felt a little touched. Her bleeding-heart thoughtfulness was kind of sweet. "As I mentioned, I have a friend or two I can dump myself on," he told her, though he hated the thought. He never liked imposing on other people's domestic situations, and he didn't know any single people without a roommate. Actually, most of his friends were married now. "It's only for another night or so, anyway."

"Really? You'll have a place you can go after that?"

"Oh, yeah."

"Well..." She paused, her brow constricting in thought. "I suppose you could stay here, since it's only a night or two. That is, if you don't mind sleeping on the balcony."

"Lanai," he corrected her. "In Hawaii they call a balcony a lanai."

"Oh." She appeared confused that he wasn't answering her question.

"I don't want to intrude on your vacation."

"We'll be seeing each other tomorrow anyway for the boat tour, so it wouldn't be an intrusion." She gazed at him matter-of-factly. "Besides, you were here all last night and I never knew the difference."

Her logical approach interested him. "But what about how it will look—you sharing a place with a strange man?"

She shrugged. "I don't know a soul here. Who would care?"

Craig was surprised. Maybe she wasn't quite as prissy as her looks and manner had led him to think.

Then her expression changed slightly and she added, "Your mother assured me that you were a fine person and someone I could trust."

Craig swallowed a chuckle. "She did?"

"I'm relying on her opinion of you."

He eyed Penelope again. She was pleasant to look at, actually rather attractive if you liked her type, and very straightforward—a trait he didn't always find in women.

But to Craig she wasn't a true temptation, and he felt he could vouch for his own trustworthiness with confidence. "I can't have you going back to Chicago telling tales to my mom," he said archly. "You can trust me."

"So, then, you're accepting my offer to stay here?"

"If you're sure you don't mind?"

"If you don't mind the lounge chair on the balcony—lanai," she corrected herself.

"The lounger is fine. It's padded and comfortable. I like sleeping in the open air."

Again her expression changed to embarrassed concern when he mentioned sleeping in the open air. She seemed to be assuming that he slept outside a lot. It occurred to Craig that she was probably offering to let him stay not only because she felt sorry for him, but perhaps also to repay Jasper's favor to her by doing what she could for his "down-and-out" son. Craig found himself tempted again out of personal pride to tell her the truth about his circumstances. He didn't really like her thinking he was penniless or even homeless. But a different kind of pride kept him from revealing any pertinent information that might get back to his father.

Later that day Jasper and Bea checked into a hotel about a mile up the coast from the condo he'd lent Penelope. Talking Bea into coming with him had been relatively easy once she'd discovered Penelope's wristband cure for motion sickness worked for her, too. Jasper had taken her on a long car ride and then they'd gone boating with a friend on Lake Michigan. Bea had been absolutely thrilled on both occasions to be able to enjoy the trips without distress.

However, when Jasper had announced that he'd like to go to Hawaii, Bea had immediately given him a suspicious look. "Yes, I want to see how things go between Penelope and Craig," Jasper had admitted. "I want to make sure they actually meet each other, just in case Penelope doesn't follow through on her promise to look him up."

"And how would you do that?" Bea had quizzed him.

"Oh, I'd find some way to throw them together."

"Jasper—"

"Aw, come on, Bea. I want to see my plan in action. Aren't you curious, too?"

"I have no intention of going there and spying on them!"

"You wouldn't have to spy," Jasper had assured her.

"Then how would we know what's happening between them?"

I'll do the spying, Jasper had thought to himself. "Kailua-Kona's not a big town, and there are only so many beaches. We'd probably catch a glimpse of him or her, or, hopefully, both of them together somewhere."

Bea had made a long sigh then. "I suppose I'd better go to keep an eye on you, in case you start carrying things too far. Besides, it's been years since I've been anywhere exotic. Now that I can manage a long plane ride with my new wristbands, I would like to go somewhere on a real vacation."

As it turned out, she had indeed managed the flight to Hawaii very well, which pleased Jasper. He liked having her along. However, there were moments he needed to be alone, too. Like now, when he wanted to call the private eye he'd hired. Bea was in the bedroom of their hotel suite, unpacking, so Jasper tiptoed to the telephone in the living room.

He dialed the number and a low male voice answered. "Lee Detective Agency. Pete Lee speaking."

"Jasper Derring. Just flew in. Have you kept track of my son, as I asked?"

"Yes, Mr. Derring, I checked his house yesterday. A workman was there redoing his floors. No sign of Craig."

"And?"

"I checked his office in town. He worked late last night and then he went home. But then he left again after a few minutes."

"Yes . . ."

"Well, I think he saw me following him. He made some maneuvers through the winding streets in the hills and . . . I lost him."

"Lost him!"

"Sorry."

"Have you seen him since?"

"He showed up at his home in the morning. Then he went to work. That's where he is now. I had to come back to my office and check on my other cases. But I'll see if I can track him better tonight."

"See that you do!" Jasper said, and hung up.

"Who was that on the phone?" Bea asked, coming into the room holding a shirt on a hanger.

"Just . . . um, wrong number."

She looked perplexed. "I didn't even hear the phone ring. Did you have to speak to them so sharply?"

"They wouldn't hang up," Jasper said, feeling a twinge of guilt for fibbing to Bea. But he knew she wouldn't approve. "Some question about my shirt?" he asked, anxious to change the subject.

"Are you really going to wear this thing? I think I should just put it back in the suitcase."

He'd gotten the shirt she was holding in the men's sportswear department at Derring Brothers. It was brightly colored with orange bird of paradise flowers against green leaves and a sky blue background. "I think it's perfect for Hawaii, Bea. That's why I picked it out."

"But, Jasper, you've never worn anything like this. You've always preferred tasteful clothes, even for casual wear."

"Why shouldn't I become more daring in my old age? Our name is Derring. We should live up to it."

Bea cocked her chin at that. "You mean, you want *me* to start wearing things like this, too?"

"Only if you want to. But I bet you'd look lovely in a nice Hawaiian blouse or dress. In fact, I think we ought go into town and do some shopping."

Bea gave him a look. "I'll shop. *You* can do the buying. I don't think, after the long flight and changing planes, and jetlag, that we should do any shopping today, though. It's late afternoon. I'm tired, and you must be, too. Remember what your doctor said about overdoing it. I think we should have a rest and then have a quiet dinner."

Jasper knew she was right. He was anxious to pursue his plans, but he'd better follow his doctor's orders. "Okay," he agreed with a sigh. "But tomorrow, we shop!"

4

The next morning Penelope saw Craig briefly when she woke up and came out of her room. He'd spent the night on her lanai. He was finishing up a piece of toast and a coffee. "I made enough coffee for both of us," he told her. "I'm leaving now, but I'll be back around two and I'll take you out on the catamaran."

"Okay," she said, still groggy from sleep. She was surprised he was up so early and wondered where he was going. Since it wasn't any of her business, she didn't ask. "See you later."

After he left, she showered and got dressed. She decided to drive south down the coast to see more of the island. The scenery was lush and exotic. She noticed colorful flowers and birds she'd never seen before. It began to rain by late morning, however. After finding a little place to eat for lunch, she returned to the condo, where the weather had remained sunny.

At 2:00 p.m., she was about to put her swimsuit and a cover-up in her canvas tote bag when Craig came in, using his key. She was surprised to see him in different clothes than the ones from yesterday, that he'd still had on when he'd left that morning. He'd shaved, too. Now he was wearing a Hawaiian-style shirt with ships, waves and clouds in its pattern, and blue walking shorts that matched rather well. So he did have some decent-looking clothes to wear. Nicely pressed, too. She wondered where he kept them.

"Ready?" he asked with a smile. Then his expression changed. "What's that?" He eyed the one-piece avocado green swimsuit she held in her hand.

"My bathing suit."

"Oh," he said, eyeing it curiously.

"I know, it's not exactly the latest style," she said with a chuckle. She'd had it since high school and had bought it to comply with the school's requirements for the swimming class everyone had to take. Bikinis and skimpy one-piece suits had not been allowed. At a sale, she and her mom had managed to find an appropriate style that fit.

Penelope felt an embarrassed need to explain why she was still hanging on to it. "I don't like to swim, and bathing suits are expensive. I didn't want to buy a new one just for this vacation, when I might never put it on anyway."

Craig set his hands on his hips, looking aghast at what she'd said. "You can't come all the way to Hawaii and never put on a swimsuit!"

His reaction miffed her. It was her vacation and her choice, wasn't it? Who was he to tell her what she could and couldn't do? On the other hand, most of her friends would probably laugh if she told them she'd been to Hawaii and never gone out in a bathing suit.

"Now that I see it, I can understand why you're reluctant to put it on." Craig shook his head. "Well, there's an easy solution—get a new one."

"A new one?" she repeated with astonishment. "But I told you, they're expensive."

"I know a place I can get you a good deal."

"You mean, you're going with me?"

"If you want the good deal."

She didn't mind a deal, but she didn't especially want him around watching her trying on swimsuits. "What about the boat trip?"

"We'll do that afterward. Come on," he said as she hesitated, "we're losing time. You drive. I'll direct you."

Before she knew it she was out the door with him, heading toward her rental car.

Jasper was standing in a Kailua-Kona clothing store, arguing with Bea over whether or not he should purchase another brightly colored Hawaiian shirt, when he happened to glance out the shop window.

"Look!" he suddenly exclaimed, pointing at a young man and woman walking down the other side of the street. "There they are! Together!"

Bea broke into a smile. "For heaven's sake! Penelope did look up Craig, as she promised. Let's go say hello."

Jasper grabbed his wife's arm to keep her from running out of the store. "No, we can't say hello! They're not supposed to know we're here."

Bea quirked her mouth. "Of course. What was I thinking? I forgot we're on a secret spying mission. I can't even say hello to my own son whom I haven't seen in two years!"

"Sometimes parents have to make sacrifices for the good of their children, Bea."

"Thank you for reminding me of my parental duty," she told him dryly.

In a hurry now, Jasper looked again at the shirt he'd taken off the rack and had been arguing about with Bea. "I think this one's perfect. It's my size. I'll take it."

"Jasper, it's red and orange and blue and absolutely gaudy. I won't want to be seen with you, if you go around wearing that."

"Then maybe you should buy one to match. They have the same pattern in women's shirts. See?" he said, pointing to a rack along the store wall.

"Have you gone totally mad?"

"No. There's method to my madness, Bea. The more we look like tasteless tourists, the less likely Craig and Penelope will recognize us if they should happen to see us. We need to buy hats and sunglasses, too. Then we can go around anywhere and not worry."

"No?" Bea arched an eyebrow. "I'll worry about getting arrested for being a public eyesore!"

"This is the place," Craig told Penelope as he guided her into a beachwear shop.

"Wow," Penelope murmured, looking intimidated by the rackfuls of swimsuits in all styles and colors.

"Hi, Craig!" Sophie greeted him. Sophie was the shop's manager, a woman in her fifties with a superb figure and spun-gold hair. Craig knew her well, because the condo he'd given up when he bought his home had been next door to hers. As his old neighbor, she'd often brought him homemade baked goods and he'd done minor repairs for her.

"Sophie." He greeted her with a smile. "This is Penelope. She's just in from Chicago, and she needs a suit."

"Fine. Two-piece or one-piece?" she asked Penelope, who looked a bit wide-eyed. "Do you know what color you'd like?"

"Well . . . one-piece. I don't know yet about color."

Sophie looked her over from head to toe with an experienced eye. "You're long-waisted. You might be more comfortable in a two-piece. Though we have one-piece suits that are made extra long for your figure type."

"Go for a two-piece," Craig said with a wink.

Penelope shot him a look. "Somehow I figured you preferred bikinis."

"Let me show you what we have," Sophie said, and led her to a corner of the store with two-piece suits.

When Sophie came back to the counter, Craig leaned toward her and said, "She's worried about the expense. Pretend you're having a half-price sale today. I'll make up the difference later, okay?"

"Sure. Is she your new girlfriend?"

"No. She's a friend of my dad's. He offered her his condo for a couple of weeks."

Sophie seemed surprised. "Are you on better terms with your dad nowadays?"

"Nope. So don't talk about my new house or my business in front of her."

"Okay. How is the new house?"

"A mess. Ned is refinishing the floors."

"It'll be beautiful when it's done, though. Going to throw a party?"

"When I get some more furniture. Shh," Craig said, glancing at Penelope, who was walking toward them with some colorful garments in her hands.

"There's a dressing room in the corner you can use to try them on," Sophie said.

As Penelope turned toward the dressing room, Craig added, "Don't forget to come out and model them for us."

Penelope glanced back at him and let out a rueful sigh.

When she'd closed the dressing room door, Craig said, "She's not the outdoorsy type. Overly modest, too. Didn't even want to put on a suit."

Sophie laughed. "You'll get her shipshape in no time."

The comment took Craig off guard. "I don't care what shape she's in. My dad told her to look me up for a boat tour. I'd just like her to get the full Hawaii experience while she's here—even get her *in* the water, if I can, for some snorkeling. Broaden her experience a little, that's all."

Sophie laughed again in a more earthy way. "You could broaden her experience quite a bit, I'm sure. I remember the string of girls coming in and out of your place."

Craig looked at her askance. "That's not what I'm up to. Really. She's not my type. She's a nice, but sort of sheltered, city girl. She doesn't have a clue what the rest of the world is like."

Both turned then as the dressing room door opened. Penelope came out hesitantly, tying a short blue, brown and beige cape-skirt around her hips that matched the bikini she was wearing. Craig found himself catching his breath. Her skin was like ivory, as if she'd never seen the sun, and her body was smooth, slender, and unusually graceful. Her shoulders and collarbone looked delicate and feminine. Her breasts, though small, plumped above the tight bikini top exquisitely. She certainly had potential, Craig thought to himself. Some guy somewhere was missing out.

"That looks wonderful on you!" Sophie exclaimed. "You picked just the right colors. The blue matches your eyes and the brown and beige blends well with your hair."

Penelope nodded. "I'm used to working with colors, so I thought it would compliment me. It's just...well, it's a little skimpy."

"Not really. For a two-piece, that's one of our more modest styles," Sophie assured her. "And you have the little skirt for a cover-up."

"It doesn't cover much," Penelope said, tugging on the skirt. She glanced at Craig.

"Covers enough for me," he said with a grin. "I think you should go for it!"

Penelope shot him another of her amused but disapproving looks, which Craig was beginning to enjoy.

"It's awfully expensive," she said. "I saw the price tag. A hundred dollars just isn't in my budget."

"We're having a half-price sale, today only," Sophie quickly told her. "We're overstocked."

"You are?" Penelope glanced around the store. "I didn't see the sign."

"Oh, for Pete's sake, I forgot to make one," Sophie said. "The older I get, the more forgetful I am." She laughed. "It's yours for fifty."

"Gosh, really?" Penelope looked pleased. "I can't pass that up! I notice you have some shorts and tops. Are they on sale, too?"

"Sure," Sophie said. As Penelope moved over to a rack on the other side of the store, Sophie eyed Craig and whispered, "If any other customers come in while she's here, you know I'll have to give them half price, too."

"I'll cover it," Craig said. "Looks like she's getting into shopping. I don't want to stop her."

He looked toward the shop's open door to see if there were any other customers on their way. A couple in straw hats and bright shirts, who apparently had been peeking in, hurried off. Craig had the feeling he'd scared them somehow.

He walked over to Penelope. "How about this?" He picked up a cutoff coral-colored T-shirt that left the midriff bare. "Lots of women wear these. They look great—especially on the slim gals."

Penelope looked doubtful. "You think so? Doesn't the wind blow it up?"

Craig paused at the question. "I don't know. *I've* never seen it happen—and I would have noticed."

"I'm sure you would have," Penelope said with a knowing grin. She took the garment from him. "Okay, I'll try it. Might as well try the matching shorts, too." As she reached around him to take the coral shorts off the rack, her shoulder brushed his chest.

Craig quickly backed away. He wasn't sure why. Somehow she'd gotten a little too close for comfort. After she'd taken hold of the shorts, she also backed away, as if having the same reaction. She kept her eyes lowered and turned to keep on browsing through the beachwear.

"Tank tops look good, too," he suggested in a purposely nonchalant way to hide his momentary discomfiture. "And short shorts."

"They may look good," Penelope said doubtfully, "but they're not exactly my style."

"Try changing your style. You have a boyfriend?"

She snuck a look at him. "No, not at the moment. Why?"

"Follow my advice and that'll change fast," he bragged.

She chuckled at his teasing. "You'll have me attracting some hotshot who'll get me in hot water!"

"That would be a feat," Craig said. "I can't even get you in cold water."

Penelope laughed so hard, her shoulders shook. She had a sense of humor about herself, Craig thought. A nice trait.

"Okay, I'll try these on," she said, now carrying a small armload of clothes.

In a few minutes she came out of the dressing room again, wearing the cutoff top and matching shorts. Craig had to admit, she looked borderline sexy. Maybe even over the border.

Sophie exclaimed how good she looked. "You should model these kinds of clothes."

"See, didn't I tell you?" Craig said.

"Okay, I'll take this outfit, too," Penelope told Sophie.

"Try on a tank top," Craig advised.

She did as he recommended and came out in a blue one of T-shirt material with flowers printed on the front.

"Looks fabulous!" Craig told her, impressed.

Then she went in the dressing room again and came out in short shorts and a black, skin-tight tank top that was cut on the low side. This one she was wearing without a bra. He could tell, because he could see the points of her nipples in the clinging knit fabric. He meant to say some words of approval, but he seemed to have lost his voice. Instead, he gave her a thumbs-up sign.

"Well, this is it, then," Penelope said. "I can't afford any more, even at half price."

She returned to the dressing room, leaving Craig to catch his breath and his wits.

"She's really pretty, isn't she?" Sophie said, eyeing him.

"Yeah, as it turns out."

"You're becoming a real-life Pygmalion," she told him with a sly grin. "You know, the *My Fair Lady* story—making over a woman to suit your tastes. And then—"

Craig shook his head. "There's no 'and then.' I'm just helping her out, like an older brother. She came here all by herself. I just want her to have some fun. I told you, she's not my type."

"She is a lot different than the sort of young women I've seen you with. But she's begun to look more like them since she came in here and you started picking out clothes for her."

"No, I'm not—she picked out her own bathing suit, didn't she?"

Penelope came back out, but instead of the bermuda shorts and T-shirt she'd walked into the store wearing, she had on the coral outfit. "I think I'll wear this. Maybe you could put my old clothes in a bag?"

"Be happy to." Sophie rang up her purchases at half price and slipped them into bags that she handed to Penelope.

"Oh, I almost forgot," Penelope said. "Do you have any bathing caps?" She realized she'd need one in case she did decide to go in the water.

"Bathing caps?" Sophie repeated. "I do, but it's mostly older women who buy them. Why would you want one?"

"A bathing *cap?*" Craig said, unsure what she was talking about.

"Those rubber things that cover up your hair and keep it from getting wet," Penelope said. "My hair is so much trouble to comb and dry."

"Why don't you get it cut?" Craig suggested.

"Cut?" Penelope looked horrified.

"You've got a lot of hair. If there's less of it, then getting it wet won't be such a problem."

"Take her over to Jeannie's," Sophie said. "She'll know the right haircut to give her."

"Huh?"

"Oh, she's just up the street, dear," Sophie assured Penelope. "Lots of us in town go to her. She's marvelous."

"Great idea," Craig said. He took Penelope's parcels from her. "Come on. We're off," he said, heading for the door. "Thanks, Sophie!"

"But... I don't want to get my hair cut..."

"Look, Bea. There they go. Let's follow."

"Jasper—"

"It's okay. He didn't recognize us. They'll never know."

"I certainly hope not. Whatever would Craig think of me dressed like this?" Bea lamented.

"I think you look cute! Let's go before we lose them."

"Look, it's one thing to help me pick out clothes, but it's a whole other thing to make me cut my hair!" Penelope was telling Craig as they walked up the street.

"Okay, okay. Sorry if I seemed high-handed. But you could at least ask Jeannie for advice. Maybe she'll know some way to handle your hair so it won't be a problem swimming. She's a friend. She won't mind."

Penelope calmed down. "Well, all right. Is it far?"

"Just around the corner."

He took her down a cross street to a small storefront with steps to one side leading upstairs. She saw a sign above that read Jeannie's Clip And Snip. The name of the place sounded ominous.

They climbed the steps and walked in. A tall brunette in her thirties wearing a beautiful flowered muumuu was blow-drying someone's hair. "Hello, Craig!"

"Hi. My friend here needs some advice."

"Okay, be with you in a minute."

Penelope sat down to wait. Craig took the seat next to her. His close proximity made her feel terribly feminine—just as she'd felt when she'd brushed against him in the store. And now, with her bared abdomen and short shorts, she felt not only feminine, but a little dangerous. It was a curious feeling she'd never experienced before, but she was beginning to like it. Once she'd tried on the bikini and hadn't gotten laughed at by Sophie or Craig, she'd gained confidence with each new thing she'd put on. The black tank top she'd bought was downright revealing, even more so than the bikini. But something had come over her and she'd decided, *What the heck? Go for it!* as Craig liked to say. Maybe he was a bad influence, she worried. She'd better be careful and watch herself. On the other hand, she'd been careful all her life. She was on vacation now. Why not do exactly what she felt like doing for a change?

Jeannie finished with her other customer in about ten minutes and motioned for Penelope to sit in the vacated barber's chair situated in front of a large mirror. Craig followed, standing next to Jeannie behind the chair. Penelope could see them both looking at her in the mirror.

"My hair is so thick, it's hard to comb through and dry," Penelope told the beautician.

"That's her excuse for not going snorkeling on my catamaran," Craig added wryly.

"There's no excuse for not snorkeling," Jeannie said with a smile. "Well, you can try braiding it, so you don't get windblown on the boat, but it'll still get wet if you go in the water. Have you thought of cutting it?"

"No."

"Yes," Craig said at the same time Penelope answered.

Jeannie laughed. "Which is it, yes or no?"

"He's trying to talk me into cutting it," Penelope said.

"That's a new one!" Jeannie looked at Craig with surprise. "Men usually like long hair."

"Sure, long hair looks nice on a pillow," he said. "But if it hinders a woman from going out and doing things, then I say, get rid of it!"

Long hair looks nice on a pillow? Penelope thought to herself, slightly shocked. It wasn't hard to guess what ruled Craig's mind! And he was Jasper and Bea's son? Must be a throwback to some earlier generation when men were men and women got dragged around by their hair. If he was going to be staying with her in the condo for a few days, maybe she'd better get her hair cut, just to be on the safe side!

"What are you smiling about?" Craig asked, eyeing her face curiously in the mirror.

Penelope gave him a puckish look. "Nothing. I've decided to go ahead and have it cut." She shifted her gaze to Jeannie. "But not too short. Later on, if I decide to grow it back, I don't want it to take years."

"How about to the middle of your neck?" Jeannie suggested, demonstrating with her hands. "You've got a nice long neck—it should look very good. And you have a natural curl. I'll layer it, so you can just let it air dry, if you want, and it'll take shape on its own. Or you can blow-dry it smooth."

"Sounds fine," Penelope said. She glanced at Craig. His expression was one of happy astonishment, as if he hadn't expected her to go along with his idea so easily. She hoped he didn't have other ideas he'd now expect her to be "easy" about.

Jeannie washed and cut her hair, then blew it dry. As Penelope watched her new style take shape in the mirror, at first she thought her neck looked too naked and her shoulders looked bare. But as her hair got fluffed and then smoothed by the beautician's brush and dryer, she began to look surprisingly sophisticated.

When Jeannie was finished, she handed Penelope a mirror and turned her swivel chair so she could see the back. Penelope studied her sleek, shining hairstyle and glanced up at Craig.

"What do you think?" she asked.

"Amazing," he said. "You look...liberated. From the weight of your hair, I mean." But he looked as if he might have meant more than that. Penelope wasn't able to penetrate his quizzical expression.

They left the salon and walked back to the main street. Penelope glanced at her watch. "Isn't it getting too late to go out on the catamaran this afternoon?"

"It's never too late," he said. "Are you chickening out on me again?"

"No. But it's past four-thirty. By the time we get on the boat and all—"

"Okay," he said, acquiescing with amusement. "But tomorrow morning's D day. No more excuses."

"Well, I *was* all set to go today," she reminded him, "but you made me go shopping and get my hair cut."

"All my fault," he agreed. "It's just as well. Snorkeling's better in the morning anyway. The water is more clear."

"Snorkeling? I only asked for a boat ride."

"And let that great bikini go to waste?"

She smiled and shook her head. "No wonder your father thought you were a problem child! You're incorrigible."

"I'm sure my dad can come up with more colorful words than that to describe me," Craig said dourly, his humorous mood disappearing.

The change in his demeanor surprised her. There must be a serious rift between Jasper and Craig, she was beginning to realize. Actually, now that she thought of it, they were a lot alike. Jasper had talked her into going to Hawaii, and now Craig was talking her into going snorkeling with the same brand of insistent charm Jasper had used. Maybe their similar personality was the root of their problem.

"I'm starting to get hungry," Penelope said. "I had an early lunch. I guess I'm still on Chicago time." She looked up at him as he walked beside her. "Since you took me shopping, how about if I buy us dinner somewhere?"

His eyes widened. "I can't remember the last time a woman bought *me* dinner. Sure, I'll take you up on that."

She smiled and said, "Good," but his reply puzzled her. She'd assumed he'd been living off of a girlfriend who had cast him aside, since at the moment he had no place to stay. But now he'd said he couldn't remember a female offering him dinner. It didn't add up. Maybe she'd made the wrong assumption about him. But he *had* been homeless and hungry when he'd shown up at Jasper's condo. And he seemed to have plenty of time on his hands, as if he didn't have steady work. On the other hand, where did the nice clothes he was wearing today come from? He was an interesting mystery, but Penelope reminded herself that his personal life was none of her business.

She noticed Craig had turned around to look behind them, and when he faced forward again, he had an incredulous expression on his face. "I've seen lots of silly-looking tourists in my line of work, but the couple walking behind us takes the cake."

Penelope turned her head surreptitiously to catch a glance. She saw an older couple about a block behind them wearing matching bright Hawaiian shirts, wide-brimmed straw hats and big sunglasses. Chuckling, she turned forward again. "They've overdone the island look, haven't they? They're missing cameras around their necks, though."

Craig blinked. "You're right, they are. It's odd, but I noticed them earlier today, too. They were peeking in the shop when you were looking at clothes. Think they're following us?"

"Why would they be following us? Do you recognize them?"

"No. Maybe I'm getting paranoid," Craig said, looking a little troubled. "Sometimes I think I see a guy in a white car tailing me when I'm driving."

Penelope grew rather alarmed. "Tailing you? Why? Does someone have a grudge against you or something?" She wondered what type of activities Craig might have gotten involved in to make ends meet.

"I don't think so."

"You seem to have a lot of friends in town," she said, thinking of Sophie and Jeannie. All of them female, too.

"I have friends all over the island. I've lived here for over a decade. As far as I know, I don't have any enemies. Maybe I'm only imagining that people are following me," he said in a breezier tone.

"That must be it," Penelope agreed. "Where should we eat?"

"There's a really good seafood place on the edge of town. I know the owner. Let's go back to the car, and I'll direct you."

They arrived at the restaurant just after five. Craig introduced her to the owner when he came to the table to

say hello to Craig. They had a pleasant dinner of mahi-
mahi on the restaurant's terrace overlooking the ocean.
Craig began telling her about the various types of fish she
would see if she went snorkeling, naming and describing
them. He especially enjoyed repeating the Hawaiian
name of one—*Humuhumunukunukuapua'a*—though
when she asked him to spell it, he got tangled up in the
letters and had to write it down for her.

"It has an easier name," he told her, handing her the
paper coaster he'd written on. "The Picasso Triggerfish,
because of its angular shape and brushstroke colors."

"I have to admit, you're making me curious to try
snorkeling. But I'm afraid I'll drown attempting to follow some fish around."

"I won't let you drown," he assured her, sounding very
confident. "You can wear a life jacket, or use a float
board, or both, if you want."

"I'll think about it."

Later, when she asked for the check, she learned that
the restaurant was having an early bird special, so the bill
was only half what she'd expected. The restaurant was
somewhat expensive, and she was happily surprised. But
it amazed her that in Hawaii people didn't seem to bother
with putting up signs to advertise their specials.

Craig thanked her for dinner and they began walking
through the restaurant to leave. On their way to the door,
she whispered to him, "Look, there at the corner table—that same older couple with the matching Hawaiian shirts and hats."

Craig took a startled glance at them. "Quick," he said
as if half joking, half serious, "let's split!"

They got into her rental car and drove back to the
condo.

* * *

"Can you see them?" Jasper asked Bea, keeping an eye on the road while trying to catch a glimpse of Penelope's rental car up ahead.

"Oh, I'm not good at this sort of thing." Bea stretched her neck forward to see out the front window. "You let all these cars get between us and them."

"I didn't want them to notice us."

"Honestly," Bea said, in an uncharacteristic complaining mood, "I couldn't see what I was eating because you made us keep our sunglasses on in the restaurant, and then I couldn't even finish my meal, because we had to race out when you saw them leave. This vacation you promised me isn't turning out to be much fun."

"There, is that them?" he asked, straining to see a car turning off the road. "I think it is! And you know what—that's our condo building, where Penelope's staying. She's taking him home with her!" Jasper congratulated himself on his undercover work, thinking that he was better at this than the incompetent gumshoe he'd hired. He'd fire Lee tomorrow.

"Penelope?" Bea said. "No, she's probably just inviting him up for some coffee. She's not the type who would sleep with a man she just met."

"Unless he's staying there," Jasper conjectured, remembering Lee had told him the floors were being redone at Craig's home. It was a circumstance Jasper had hoped for when he'd learned from the detective that Craig was having work done on his new house. It was why Jasper had hurried Penelope into going to Hawaii before the end of the month. He hoped Craig might decide to stay at the condo while the refurbishing was going on.

"Why would he be staying there if he has a new home?" Bea asked.

Jasper didn't reply, not wanting to reveal all he knew. He pulled into the entrance and stopped his car. They watched as Craig and Penelope disappeared around a building on their way to the condo. "There they go," Jasper said with glee. "I wish we could stay here and see when or if he leaves to go home."

"That could take all night," Bea said. "If that's what you're planning, then take me to our hotel and you can come back and do your stupid stakeout all by yourself." She fussed with her purse, looking downright upset. "Honestly, spying on your own son! What they do or don't do together is their business and not ours."

Jasper knew he should agree with Bea's sense of propriety, but his curiosity and his hopes were too strong. However, Bea seemed to be getting a little too upset, and Jasper decided he'd better start thinking about his own marital situation. He didn't want to succeed in finally marrying off all his children, only to lose his wife in the process.

"Yes, Bea, of course you're right. I get carried away, don't I? Well, we'll go back to the hotel. I've learned all I need to for now—they've met, and they seem to be getting along fine."

Jasper hoped they'd do a lot more than just get along well. He hoped Craig would indeed spend the night at the condo and that sparks would ignite between them. He even secretly hoped they'd conceive a grandchild while they were at it—but he knew he was rushing things. Bea would prefer it if they were married first.

As he turned the car around to go back to town, he heard Bea exhale a big sigh of relief. Jasper sighed, too, but in silence. He loved Bea dearly, but sometimes he wished she were a little more bohemian.

Just before ten o'clock, Craig stretched out on the lounger on the lanai to go to sleep. Penelope had gone to bed already, still on Chicago time. A party girl, she wasn't. But Craig had to admit she'd turned into a pretty flashy babe. Sophie's comment about him playing Pygmalion may have been apt after all. Nevertheless, Sophie's typically feminine notion that he'd fall for her was wishful romantic hokum.

Penelope was still a little too different from any of the women he'd been attracted to over the years. For one thing, most women in this situation—sharing a condo with him—would be in bed with him by now. Her sense of propriety reminded him of his mother's.

He recalled then that Penelope had bought that revealing black tank top, which had surprised him. But, he thought with amusement, he'd be willing to bet she'd never wear it. He had the feeling she sometimes wanted to break out of her mold but didn't have the adventurous spirit to do so. Just like Mom. Despite his father's strong, persuasive personality, his mother had never changed. In a way, Craig had to admire her for that. She'd remained true to her down-to-earth, modest self. She possessed a rare wisdom and perception, but had always been refined and cautious. He had the feeling Penelope was cut of the same cloth—at least as far as being refined and cautious.

An unsettling thought crept into Craig's mind as he looked up at the starry sky. Psychologists had a long-standing theory that a person marries someone who is like his mother.

"Stupid psycho-babble," Craig muttered. He told himself to turn off his mind and go to sleep.

But it took a long time for his mind to turn off. His thoughts kept returning to the young woman sleeping alone on the bed inside.

5

→ ←

Craig had to chuckle. Wearing wristbands for seasickness, no less, Penelope looked helplessly out of her element and totally adorable. They were aboard his smallest, oldest catamaran, which he kept for nostalgic reasons but no longer used for tourist excursions. She'd put on her new bikini, though he'd seen little of it. He'd advised her to leave on her cover-up T-shirt so her back wouldn't get burned in the sun. After finding a pair of black flippers for her feet, he'd slipped an orange life jacket over her head and fastened the attached straps around her waist. He showed her how to blow it up to the size that suited her.

"Now what?" she asked, looking as if she felt awkward. And maybe a little scared.

"Now the mask and snorkel gear," he told her, pulling them out of a storage chest built into the catamaran. He slipped the mask over her head, making sure it covered her nose, then tightened it. "Breathe in," he told her.

She tried and then seemed to panic, pulling the mask up with her hands. "I can't."

"Good."

"What do you mean, *good?*" she asked, looking at him as if he were being treacherous.

"That means it's tight enough—airtight. You breathe through your mouth with this," he said, adjusting the attached snorkel, turning the clear mouthpiece toward her face. "Bite on the mouthpiece and slip it under your lips." She cooperated warily. His fingers touched her lower lip as he held the mouthpiece for her. She had a pretty mouth, he noted—soft and yielding. He felt an unexpected rush of desire. Keeping his thoughts from straying too far, he pointed the other, long end of the snorkel upward behind her head. "The top stays above water, supplying you with air, and you breathe only through your mouth. If you keep trying to inhale through your nose, you'll get a headache."

She took out the mouthpiece. "If I don't drown first. What if water gets into the snorkel tube?"

"Then you blow it out, like a whale does when it comes to the surface. The life jacket will keep you afloat."

"How deep is the water here?" she asked, looking out at the small secluded bay he'd taken them to. It was his favorite, secret place to snorkel. Neither his tour company nor others brought tourists here. Ned had told him about the bay years ago. The locals kept the place to themselves.

"About twelve feet." He'd anchored at the same spot he always did, on coral that was already damaged, so as to preserve the coral in the rest of the bay.

"Twelve feet?" she said, aghast. "I've never been in water that deep."

"You wouldn't want your feet to touch the bottom. Coral is rough, and besides, if you touched it, it would stop growing. The idea is to float on the surface and look down at the fish below."

"But *twelve* feet? Isn't there someplace more shallow?"

"Sure, but you'll see less. This is the best spot. I can give you a float board, if that'll make you feel more secure." He lifted the lid of a large storage box and pulled out a board about a yard long made of lightweight plastic foam. "You can lie across this sideways and look over the edge with your mask in the water."

Penelope eyed it with hesitation. "If you say so."

"Come on, let's go." He pulled on his flippers, grabbed his own mask and snorkel, and assisted her down the short flight of built-in metal steps that led down into the water from the back of the catamaran. He went first, pushing himself into the gentle waves. Penelope followed, holding on to the railing for dear life, looking like a scared duckling in her big flippers. She reached the last rung below the surface, but held on and would not let go.

"Just step into the water. You'll float. Come on, I'll hold on to you."

He could see her grimacing behind the mask, her eyes wide with fear. She put the mouthpiece back into her mouth, as if readying herself. After a few long seconds she finally stepped off. He held the float board steady while she pulled herself up onto it. Then a small wave came and she slipped off. He helped her try again. Eventually, she got herself balanced correctly and was able to stay on the board, which was under her chest, with her arms and hands in a death grip on the edge of the board.

He encouraged her to put her face in the water, reminding her to breathe through the tube in her mouth. She did this tentatively, but soon seemed transfixed by what she was seeing below the surface.

"Ready for a tour of the bay?" he asked. "I'll hold on to your float board and pull you around."

She lifted her head and nodded. After slipping his own mouthpiece into place, he took hold of her board and swam away from the catamaran toward a rocky outcrop where he'd always found the most fish.

Penelope eagerly looked through her mask at the undersea world below. She saw pink coral and, further on, yellow coral, with fish of many varieties and colors darting here and there, sometimes alone, sometimes in whole schools, crossing each other's paths, their bright colors shining in the sunlight that filtered through the water. All at once a sea turtle appeared from under a rock and swam below them on its way to some other spot.

Craig tapped her arm to get her attention. She took her face out of the water and turned to him.

He pulled the mouthpiece from between his teeth to speak. "There's a Picasso Triggerfish. The one with the odd shape and long smile."

Long smile? she thought, looking back into the water. She searched the direction in which he'd pointed. Soon she saw a curious-looking fish vaguely in the shape of a triangle with the mouth, tail and stomach making up the three points. Its mouth at the front tip was small, but a yellow line that changed to orange went back from its mouth, making it look as if it was smiling. It had blue lines straight down from its small eye and the rest of it had an artistic pattern of green, blue and orange against a pale background. She remembered at the restaurant he'd described the fish as looking as if it had brushstrokes. No wonder they'd named it after Picasso, for it resembled a piece of modern art.

She lifted her face from the water and extracted her mouthpiece. "I saw it! It's neat!"

"The black-and-yellow-striped ones are Moorish Idols," he told her.

She quickly moved to put the mouthpiece back in her mouth, but a wave came as she did so, and since she didn't have a good grip, she slipped off the float board. "Oh!" she exclaimed before she could get the mouthpiece back in place. She found herself floating on her back because of the life jacket, flailing around.

Craig caught the float board, brought it back to her and held it steady while she pulled herself onto it again. "Thanks," she said, out of breath.

"Okay, now?"

"Yes."

"Have you had enough?" he asked.

"No!"

"That's my girl! Got your snorkel back in place?"

She slid the mouthpiece, salty tasting from the water, into her mouth and nodded to him to proceed.

They stayed out at least another forty-five minutes, floating all over the small bay, until Craig got her attention and said, "We've been out over an hour. That's probably about enough for your first time. I'll head us back to the catamaran, okay?"

She nodded in agreement, feeling disappointed at having to stop, but her arms were getting sore from holding on and her mouthpiece was beginning to get uncomfortable.

Soon they arrived at the steps of the catamaran. As she grabbed hold of the rail, he took the float board from her and helped push her up to take the first step. The waves had picked up and getting a grip on the rail wasn't easy. Soon, with his support, she'd pulled herself out of the sea. Dripping with salt water, she stepped up onto the boat.

Craig followed, taking off his own mask and flippers. He helped her remove her gear and the life jacket.

"Take off your wet T-shirt," he told her. As she did so, he grabbed some large, clean white towels from somewhere and handed her one. She slipped it around her shoulders.

Penelope watched him dry himself off, his broad, well-developed chest and shoulders glistening in the sun. She'd noticed his physique earlier, when he'd pulled off his shirt to get ready to snorkel. For a few minutes it had almost distracted her from her trepidation about going in the ocean. But when he told her she'd be stepping into water twelve feet deep, she'd forgotten all about his magnificent chest, more worried about surviving her first snorkeling adventure.

As he dried his lean, muscular thighs and legs, the towel brushed the manly bulge under his blue bathing trunks. Penelope forced herself to glance away. He might look good enough for one of those beefcake calendars, he might be absolute ecstasy in bed, but a steady income would probably always elude him. And marriage probably wasn't in his plans, either. However tempting he might be, he wasn't the sort of man she ultimately was hoping to meet.

On the other hand, she'd never experienced absolute ecstasy in bed....

Never mind! she instructed herself, tossing her towel onto a nearby seat and running her hands through her hair.

"See?" he said, watching her. "Your hair hardly even got wet."

"I know," she said, pleasantly surprised. "Just on the ends."

"The float board kept you buoyed up. Next time, you should try it without the board, though. It's easier to move around and more comfortable."

"I wish the snorkel mouthpiece was more comfortable," she said, rubbing the sides of her mouth with her fingers. "My lip muscles are sore from holding it in place."

She glanced up to find his eyes focused on her mouth in an absorbed gaze.

"There's a cure for that." His tone had changed, growing low and almost whispery.

"A cure?" she repeated, mesmerized by his voice and eyes, yet suspecting what he meant.

"Lip massage," he murmured, and the next thing she knew his hands were taking hold of her upper arms, pulling her close. Suddenly his lips fastened onto hers with purpose and obvious pleasure. His mouth felt warm and insistent, yet he took his time, enjoying himself. Her knees began to feel weak.

When he let go, she said breathlessly, "Is that part of your tour package?"

"No. That's for free."

She grinned at his nonchalant audacity, not wanting to look as helplessly rattled as she felt. "You seem to know your way around boats *and* women."

"That's accurate," he said. "Though you're sort of a new make and model for me."

"Well, don't think about trying to break me in," she told him, tossing her hair back.

His eyes seemed to catch fire as he watched her raise her chin. Her heart began to beat faster. This was unexpected and strange. Why was he coming on to her all of a sudden? Or did he just behave this way automatically whenever he was alone with a woman on a boat?

"Better put on some sunscreen," he said, stepping away from her. "Whatever you'd put on before would have washed off." He took a tube out of a sports bag he'd brought on board with him. After squeezing some onto his fingertips, he reached out and playfully dabbed some on her nose.

She laughed and began spreading the white goo over her face. When she'd finished he squeezed some more into her hand. He watched, looking positively fascinated as she spread it over her upper arm, moving her hand downward in long strokes. The way he observed her so closely made her feel feminine and sexy.

"You're so pale," he said, shaking his head slightly. She couldn't tell if his comment was in disapproval, or if it was a compliment. He squeezed some more sunscreen onto his fingers and moved behind her. She felt his hand glide slowly over her shoulders and down her back, spreading the cream. She closed her eyes at the warm, exploring sensitivity she felt in his touch.

"Is this another free service for your customers?" she asked, trying to sound flip and not faint with pleasure.

He stopped, removing his hands from her. "No, just trying to be helpful. You want to do this yourself?" He held the tube out for her to take.

"It might be safer." Penelope took the tube, yet felt deprived now that he'd stopped touching her.

"Safer?"

She turned to face him. "I just came here to snorkel, not to..."

"What?"

"Get carried away with other things."

"Maybe I misread you," he said, sounding a bit arch now. "When you came out of the water you looked exhilarated. There was a glow in your eyes. You gazed at me in a certain way when I was toweling myself off. I thought—"

"Yes, you have a great body," she interrupted him, not wanting to hear what he'd assumed. "I'll admit I find you attractive. But that doesn't mean that I'm ready to...to..."

"Get aroused?"

"Yes. No! Do you have to be so blunt? You shouldn't be talking to me this way. Your mother said I could trust you, remember?"

He lowered his eyes, a resigned smile on his lips. "You would have to remind me of my mom. Well, that burst the bubble."

"Bubble? What bubble?"

"For a few minutes there I thought we had a mutual attraction going. I forgot about reality, about the fact that you're friends with my parents." He tilted his head, looking amused in a bitter way. "But it's just as well you reminded me. You're right, we'd better avoid getting each other aroused with suntan lotion. It's a bad idea."

"You mean," she said with hesitance, knowing she shouldn't be asking, "you find me...attractive?"

His expression grew muddled, changing from bitterness to something just short of confusion. "When I first met you, I never expected to. You were prissy... fragile...no sense of adventure. But look at you now— you do damn fine justice to that bikini. Your haircut makes you look sassy instead of shy. And you braved the deep waters with me and had a great time snorkeling."

She smiled self-consciously as he reminded her of the change in herself. "Looks like you turned me into a beach bum's babe."

She was happy to see him laugh again. "What am I?" he asked. "The beach bum? Is that how you see me?"

His questions embarrassed her, and she wished she hadn't made the comment. "I was just joking. Don't take it personally."

Before she could think, she found herself swept into his arms again. "I'll try not to," he said, holding her securely against his warm chest, nuzzling her forehead with his nose. "You're turning out to be an adorable, intriguing woman. In many ways we're mismatched, but maybe we should explore the possibilities anyway."

"W-what possibilities?" she said, feeling deliriously suffocated against him.

"I think we should let ourselves get aroused and see what happens," he said, sliding his cheek against hers and biting her earlobe.

"I didn't come to Hawaii with the intention of having a . . . a wild fling," she said, her shoulders scrunching at the sensation of his lips on her neck.

"Better a wild fling than a mediocre one."

She laughed, but when he tried to kiss her, she made a halfhearted effort to push herself away. "I didn't want to have any kind of fling," she told him, chuckling as she tried to avoid his mouth. "I'm serious."

"You don't sound serious," he teased.

"But really," she said, trying to put on a more sober expression. "I don't do that. I don't have one-night stands and things like that."

"You're a virgin?"

She half smiled in a wry manner. "Why? Do you think I look like one?"

"Not now."

"No, I'm not a virgin. Years ago I had a relationship with someone I hoped I'd wind up married to. But it didn't work out."

He studied her with bright curiosity in his eyes. "How come?"

"I . . . sort of got bored with him. He was a good man. A banker. I really should have married him. He truly cared for me. But . . ."

"You broke his heart?"

"Yes, I guess so," she said with a sense of sadness. "I didn't mean to. He wanted to set a wedding date, and I just couldn't make myself commit. So I broke off with him."

"Any other shattered men in your past?" Craig asked.

"No. I learned to recognize sooner if I'd really be attracted to them. I dated other men, but never . . . you know . . . got intimate."

"And how old are you?"

"Twenty-eight. Well, almost twenty-nine."

"And you've never had a wild fling?"

"Well, not . . . no." She studied him, his amused eyes, handsome face, the sun-bleached hair brushing his forehead in the sea breeze. "But if you think I'm going to have one with you, because you make eyes at me and apply sun cream with a deft touch, then . . ."

"Then, what?"

"You're . . . mistaken." She wished she sounded more sure of her conviction.

"Deft touch?" he repeated, ignoring her answer to his question. "You want me to finish the job?"

"No . . ."

He held her closer, running his hands over her bared waist and torso. "I won't miss a spot," he said, kissing her chin.

"I'll bet." She laughed helplessly when he blew in her ear. "You use every trick, don't you? Do the girls all fall for this 'blow in her ear and she'll follow you anywhere' routine?"

To her surprise, he took her by the shoulders and gave her a shake. She looked up to find his expression had grown more serious again. "I don't usually have to use any tricks," he said. "I guess that's what I like about you. You're a challenge. I'm just doing the best I can to charm you."

Charm he had in spades, she thought to herself. So he saw her as a challenge. She had to admit, this was the most excitement she'd had in years. Maybe ever. He made her feel alive again. He made her feel like a desirable woman. She'd forgotten how it felt.

She chewed her lip, which drew his attention. She loved the way he studied her every move. A fling would be going too far, she told herself, but...maybe she could at least have a little harmless fun. "Okay," she said blithely. "You can finish applying the sunscreen."

His eyes narrowed quizzically and little mischievous lights played in them. "Fine," he said, barely hiding his smile. He squeezed out more lotion and began on her other arm. Using long, languid strokes, he rubbed it into her skin. Next he worked on her abdomen and stomach, his touch making her skin quiver. She began to breathe faster. He moved behind her and applied it to her lower back, above her bikini line, moving upward, slipping his hand beneath the back of her bikini top. And then all at once, he unfastened it.

She gasped and stood still, knowing she should object. But she didn't. He continued spreading the cream over her back and down her side, then upward again beneath the opened bikini top. He stepped closer and she felt his chest against her back, warm, solid, and masculine. As she held her breath, sensing what was coming, she felt his hand slide forward over her breast. His fingertips found her nipple.

"Oh, why?" she murmured, an ache in her voice. "Don't do *this* to me."

He slid his other hand over her other breast, firmly yet gently fondling her softness. "Do you want me to stop?"

She squeezed her eyes shut. It had been years since any man had touched her this way. And it had never felt like this. She couldn't find the voice to answer him.

When she didn't respond, one of his hands slipped away and she felt a tug on the bikini strap tied at the back of her neck. All at once the top fell off, landing at her feet.

He wrapped his arms around her, his inner forearms covering her breasts as he embraced her with surprising passion. "You're so sexy," he breathed in her ear before kissing her hotly at the side of her neck.

All at once he spun her around and, placing his hands below the back of her waist, pulled her pelvis against his. He gazed at her naked breasts, devouring her with his eyes. "God, you're exquisite." Bending to kiss her shoulder, he slowly slid his mouth along her skin over the rise of her breast. His lips fastened onto the contracting nub of her nipple.

She gave a little cry when he sucked hard. "No..." she said in a wanton whimper.

He raised his head, nuzzling her cheek. "Tell me when you want me to stop."

"You're too good at this," she weakly confessed, closing her eyes at the sublime feel of her breasts sliding against his heated chest. His temperature was definitely rising. When his lips claimed hers in a torrid, jubilant manner, she grew dizzy, but kissed him back with all she could muster. Then his pelvis nudged her in a conscious, urgent way. She felt his hardness. A pulse of desire and anxiety shot through her.

"Right here," he whispered roughly, his hands sliding over her skin toward her bikini bottom. "Right now."

All at once she came to her senses. "This is madness. We can't do this!" she exclaimed, pushing away from him, shocked at how far she'd let things go. "I hardly know you. And we don't have any protection—I don't want to come home from my vacation pregnant!" Her trembling hand rose to her lips, still burning from his kisses. "My God, you're Jasper's *son*. I was just supposed to look you up, not have sex with you!"

Craig was staring at her, looking stunned, breathing raggedly. But when she mentioned his father, he quickly sobered and his whole posture grew reserved. He brushed his eye with his fingers and then directed his gaze to the ocean's horizon. "You're right. You're right. Sorry. I don't know how I . . . what I was thinking. I got carried away, that's all. It's been a while since I've been with a woman."

As she picked up her bikini top to put it back on, she felt rather deflated at his explanation. For a few mindless moments he'd made her believe she had been the reason for his sudden passion. But apparently he simply hadn't had sex lately and she was handy. Any woman in a bikini would probably have turned up his furnace. And what a furnace! she thought as her shaky fingers fumbled trying to fasten her top back in place. She knew it would have been extremely foolish, but she found herself half wishing she hadn't stopped him. Now she'd never know. . . .

* * *

My God, what got into me? Craig asked himself as he went to the wheel of the catamaran to head back home. He kept forgetting she was a friend of his father's. That was reason enough to leave her alone, but he also had the strong suspicion that she and he were victims of his dad's matchmaking scheme. Starting an affair with her would be just about the most vacant-headed thing he could do—especially without a condom. He'd always been careful about that, leery of becoming a father. How had he turned stupid all of a sudden?

Penelope was so ingenuous, almost wide-eyed some-times—and at others, surprisingly playful—that more and more he found himself fixated with curiosity when-ever he was near her. That same devilish curiosity had begun prodding him to explore what sort of a lover she would be.

He'd become rather jaded about women and sex the last year or so. Didn't know why—just had. But when he was around Penelope, he felt fresh and new, as if he was eighteen again. She didn't chase him. She didn't hang on his shoulder adoringly and whisper provocative things to get his attention. Penelope had a touch of class, an inner beauty he'd forgotten some women possessed. And she didn't have a clue that he was wealthy. The fact that he was Jasper Derring's son was something she viewed as an impediment. She actually thought he was a beach bum.

In one way, this was unfortunate, but in another, Craig found it a relief. He'd met so many gold diggers in his life. Even island women who didn't know he was a mil-lionaire's son had guessed how successful he'd become and chased him constantly. Penelope seemed to be at-tracted to him for himself—he didn't think he'd imag-ined her sensual response. She presented an appealing respite for him from the predatory babes he'd begun to avoid.

Too bad he couldn't enjoy her company more. But common sense needed to prevail at this point. He was damned fortunate she'd stopped him.

Jasper peered through his binoculars, trying to catch another glimpse of the two people on the catamaran. He was standing on a high point overlooking a small bay. Bea was next to him, enjoying the panoramic view without the aid of binoculars. Good thing, Jasper thought. He was positive it was Craig's old catamaran—he'd taken Jasper on it in years past. He'd gotten a glimpse of it from his hotel lanai as it left Kailua-Kona harbor. Noting the direction it had taken, he'd suggested to Bea that they take a ride along the coast to enjoy the scenery. After several stops at scenic pullovers, he'd finally hit paydirt when he saw Craig's catamaran in a small, almost hidden bay.

Better yet, he'd been thrilled to see a dark-haired, slim woman greatly resembling Penelope as Craig's only passenger. He'd nearly yelled *Eureka!* when he'd seen them kiss. Unfortunately, the wind had made the anchored craft shift and the cabin got in the way of his view of the embracing couple. But what he'd glimpsed had been quite enough to assure him that his plan was on track and working very well.

"What are you smiling so smugly about?" Bea asked him.

"See the boat that's disappearing around the rocks? That's Craig's catamaran."

Bea focused her gaze on the craft with interest. "Is it?"

"Yup. And guess who I saw on the boat with him?" Jasper asked, wiggling the binoculars in his hand.

"Penelope?" Bea said with a disbelieving smile.

"You got it! I think we'd better start planning for another wedding."

"Jasper, she said she'd ask him to take her on a boat excursion as a favor to us, remember? You can't assume they're ready to get married just because—"

He leaned toward his wife and said quietly near her ear, "They were kissing. I saw them!"

"No, really?" Bea said, her hazel eyes lighting up with surprise.

"Saw it with my own eyes," Jasper assured her.

"Well, it's a romantic setting. Maybe they got carried away by the moment."

"Nonsense," Jasper said. "A kiss is a kiss."

"You remind me of that song from *Casablanca*—a kiss is just a kiss. It's the fundamental things that apply, Jasper. And one kiss doesn't mean we should run back into town and hunt for wedding presents."

Jasper took in a long breath and held his tongue. No use arguing. Bea just didn't seem to get the hang of positive thinking.

By midafternoon Penelope had returned to Jasper's condo, alone. Craig had brought the catamaran back to Kailua-Kona and had told her he had things to do in town. When she'd asked if he'd need a ride later, he'd told her no. She thought his car—she assumed he had one—was still at Jasper's condo, but she wasn't sure. As she'd driven back by herself, she'd wondered if he'd stay at her place tonight or find somewhere else to go.

Before going up, she'd stopped at the little store near the complex to buy some more milk and some sandwich meats. She might be eating at home tonight. As she'd passed by the store's small drugstore section, she'd noticed boxes of condoms displayed. Impulsively, she'd picked one up. She'd glanced away when the store clerk rang up her purchases.

Now, as she unpacked the small bag of groceries on the kitchen table, she came across the condoms. She chuckled at herself and wondered why she'd wasted the money. It was probably wishful thinking that had made her pick them up. She doubted Craig would be back after what had happened on the boat. He'd steer clear of *her* from now on. He'd even apologized, which only indicated that he'd regretted what had happened, too.

And why should she want to make love with him anyway, if he was only looking for a handy female to ease his needs? She sighed. Why? Because he was so handsome and so good with his lips and hands, he'd made her head swim. What an experience it would be! All her life, since she was a teenager, she'd wondered what great sex would be like. If she continued in her usual pattern of staying away from the ne'er-do-well charmers she found so attractive, and trying to make it work with the Steady-Eddy types who didn't turn her on, she'd never find out.

Maybe she shouldn't have stopped Craig. After all, she was on vacation, far from home. No one would ever know she'd let herself become temporarily "easy." And once she returned home, she could fall back into her usual life pattern—only she'd have had a great memory to live on for the rest of her life. Oh, why hadn't she let him take her, right there on the boat, all hot and impetuous and full of lust as they were?

She looked down at the box of condoms in her hand. Well, for one thing, she might indeed have gotten pregnant. On second thought, she decided with another sigh, she'd been absolutely right to stop him. Why did life have so many heavy-duty consequences? Ruefully, she turned

the box over in her hands. *Now* she was prepared. Oh, for
a second chance! Would Craig come back tonight?

Even if he did return, she'd probably get all sensible
again and decide against an affair. She always had the
memory of her errant dad, not to mention her long-
suffering mom, permanently in the back of her mind. She
didn't want to make the mistake of falling head-over-
heels for the wrong guy and becoming a replica of her
mother—happy only late in life when she was finally free
of men.

Twisting her mouth in a self-admonishing expression,
Penelope tossed the unopened box into the wastebasket.

6

————►◄————

Late that afternoon Craig got one of his employees at his office to drive him to his house. He'd forgotten that he'd left his Porsche at Jasper's condo. Not anxious to go over there yet, he decided to figure out some way to get it later.

Craig still felt oddly unsettled by what had happened with Penelope. Despite all those rushed moments of heated desire and heavy breathing they'd shared on the catamaran, when he'd docked, they had parted on polite but cool and awkward terms. Somehow he didn't feel right about how they'd left things, yet he didn't know what more he should have done or said. He knew the whole incident was his fault. He shouldn't have made physical advances toward her. On the other hand, she didn't have to respond to him with all those sexy gasps and kisses. She certainly took her time about pushing him away. He wasn't used to women who sent such mixed messages.

All afternoon, attending to his work, he'd felt as if he were under a gray cloud. By the end of the long day, he still hadn't been in any mood to analyze his muddled state of mind. He'd rather have just forgotten the whole thing—if he could have.

After the employee dropped him off, he went into his house and found Ned kneeling in the open doorway between the kitchen and the dining room, doing the last touches on the dining room floor. The wood in the empty room shone with rich color.

"Looks magnificent," Craig said, smiling for the first time since he'd gotten off his catamaran that morning. "Almost finished?"

"Just about," Ned replied, obviously proud of himself. "The rooms and hallway upstairs were done yesterday, and I varnished the rooms downstairs today. This is the last one."

"So, I can stay here tonight?"

Ned gave him an are-you-kidding look. "No, boss. Can't you see it's still drying? Don't you smell the fumes? You step on it, and I'll yell so loud, they'll hear me on Maui."

"Okay. I wasn't thinking," Craig said. He exhaled a long breath. "Tomorrow?"

"Yeah, probably by tomorrow night you can move back in. I'll check it in the afternoon. Push the furniture back into place for you."

"Thanks."

"Where've you been staying?" Ned asked.

"My dad's condo."

"Oh, I see." Ned seemed to understand Craig's misgivings. "Well, you can still stay with me and my family."

"I know. I don't like to impose. Besides, I left my car at the condo. I have to go back to pick it up." Craig began to mutter under his breath. "Might as well put in one more night there. Damn."

"Left your car there? Is it broken?"

"No. Someone else drove me into town this morning. It's a long story."

"A new wahine in your life?" Ned asked, his eyes twinkling.

The question took Craig off guard. "Why assume that?"

"I ran into Sophie last night, and she said you came into her shop with a classy-looking chick. Even bought her clothes. I thought, 'All *right!*' Told Sophie I was glad you were back in action—"

Craig put up his hand in a quelling motion. "It's not what you think. She's a friend of my dad's."

Ned's jubilant expression fell. "Oh."

"She's here on vacation and on a tight budget. So I quietly asked Sophie to let me pay part of her bill. It's no big deal. That's all there was to it."

"Okay. I was just hoping..."

"Hoping what?" Craig asked testily. "I don't need to have some female in tow to be happy. They're more trouble than they're worth."

"You didn't used to think so," Ned reminded him.

"Well, I've wised up."

Ned didn't seem to be listening to him, absorbed in his own thoughts. "Wait. This gal is a friend of your dad's. Wouldn't he have invited *her* to stay at his condo?"

Craig sighed, wishing his old pal would get off the subject. "Your powers of deduction are admirable."

"And you said *you're* staying at your dad's condo. So... you're staying there *with* her?"

"She uses the bedroom. I sleep on the lanai. I didn't even know she would be there. When I showed up, she...was nice enough to let me stay. That clear up all the questions buzzing around in your brain?"

"You sleep on the lanai?" Ned repeated, looking mystified. "Is she married or something?"

"No. Just because she's single, it doesn't mean she wants to sleep with me." Craig heard himself defending Penelope, and it confused him more than he felt already. He paced uneasily to the other side of the kitchen.

"Well, that's a new one," Ned said. "Must be losing your touch, boss. See, I told you. Living like a hermit here, it's not good for you. You're sliding downhill already."

"How about finishing up that floor instead of doling out advice?"

"Oh, I'm all done," Ned said, standing, a brush and cloth in his hands. "Just got to clean up."

"Thank God." While Ned cleaned his brush, Craig continued to pace the kitchen, feeling out of sorts. "When you're ready, can you drive me to my dad's condo? My car—"

"Sure, no problem. Only to pick up your car?" Ned teased. "You aren't staying there for the night—out on the lanai all by yourself?"

Craig looked up at the ceiling. If Ned wasn't such an old friend and a treasured craftsman, he'd ring his neck. "I don't know. I'm still thinking about that."

"Must give you a heap of frustration, huh?" Ned laughed.

Craig couldn't find humor in Ned's needling, because his comment was all too true.

A half hour later Ned dropped him off by his Porsche in the condo's parking lot. After Ned drove off, Craig debated his options. In the end, he found himself going up the elevator to the condo. He'd decided to have a brief talk with Penelope to clear the air, so to speak, and leave. Then maybe he could forget the whole incident.

When he got to the door, he knocked instead of using his key. She opened it and her blue eyes grew wide when she saw him. She wore bermuda shorts and a crisp camp shirt. It was a conservative outfit she'd probably brought with her from Chicago. Except for her haircut, she looked as if she'd changed back into her old, cautious self.

"Craig," she said, opening the door wider. "I wondered if you'd come back." Her demeanor was diffident and hesitant.

"I left my car here. Just came back to pick it up and . . . and sort of settle things with you. We both felt a little uneasy with each other earlier, and I didn't want there to be any hard feelings."

"Come in," she said.

"Just for a minute," he told her, walking in. When she'd closed the door, he said, "I didn't mean for all that to happen. That is, I didn't take you out on the catamaran with the plan to try to seduce you or anything like that. It's . . . I don't know, we'd had fun snorkeling and you . . . you looked great, and I forgot myself. I mean— jeez—you're a friend of my dad's. It was stupid."

He glanced at Penelope and found her looking stiff and slightly troubled, her eyes straying to the wall and to the table. "It's all right," she said, gazing in his direction yet not really looking at him. "I did have fun snorkeling. And . . . I have no hard feelings toward you. You stopped when I asked. Not every man would be such a gentleman about it as you were. So . . . to repeat, no hard feelings." She gave him a little smile that didn't quite reach her eyes.

His conscience squirmed when she called him a gentleman. If he'd been a gentleman, he wouldn't have unfastened her bikini top. His eyes strayed to her breasts, well hidden beneath the buttoned-up cotton camp shirt. And then he looked away, chiding himself for his wandering thoughts.

"Thanks," he said. "I appreciate that." God, he sounded formal. He'd wanted to clear the air, and felt he had, but the air was still thick with awkwardness between them. Neither of them seemed to feel any better. "Well, I just came to get my car, as I said. So... I hope you enjoy the rest of your stay in Hawaii."

"D-do you have a place to stay yet?" she asked, fiddling with the collar of her shirt, as if straightening it.

"I can go to a hotel. It's no problem. Besides, tomorrow night I'll have a permanent place."

"You will?" she asked, her eyes searching his more directly now than before.

"Yeah, I... um, I'm house-sitting," he said, improvising. "It's a nice, big house, so I'll be fine for a long while."

She gave him a genuine smile, her eyes crinkling. Sometimes she could have the most sincere, disarming smile he'd ever seen. "That's great! I'm glad you have a good situation now. You know, if it's just for tonight, there's no need to go to a hotel. You can stay here, on the lanai again."

He raised his eyebrows. "Thanks, but... you'd trust me?"

She swallowed and looked down. With a quick little shrug of her shoulders, she said, "I'll lock my bedroom door. I guess neither of us wants a repeat of what happened on the boat. So it's not really a matter of trust. I don't see how anything more *would* happen, at this point."

Craig nodded, uneasily agreeing with her logic. He thought a moment, or pretended to. His mind was curi-

ously empty. Then he found himself nodding again.
"Okay, if you're sure you don't mind. That works well
for me. They'd look at me oddly if I tried to check into a
hotel with no luggage."

"That's true," she agreed. "They probably would."
She glanced toward the kitchen with a wringing motion
of her hands. "Have you eaten dinner?"

He shook his head. "Not hungry. How about you?"

"Oh, I had a sandwich earlier. There's some ham and
cheese left, if you want something later. Just help yourself."

"Thanks."

She lifted her hand to her cheek, as if suddenly remembering something. "I almost forgot. I never paid
you for taking me snorkeling."

He smiled. "No charge."

"Oh, no, I want to pay you your usual fee. Please, tell
me how much it was."

He stared at her unblinking. After the way he'd kissed
her and fondled her, she was worrying about paying him?

He realized she was staring back at him, her lips parting as if in awe. Sometimes she just had no clue how sexy
she was. Bruskly, to break the unexpected moment, he
turned away. "I'll figure up my time and let you know in
the morning. Okay?"

"Sure."

There was silence for a long moment. He risked a
glance at her. She was pushing her hair back from her
face. Her hand, he noticed, was trembling. Their mutual stare had affected her, too. Craig was beginning to
realize he may have made a mistake agreeing to stay here
with her one more night. But it was too late to change his
mind. To abruptly say he was leaving might hurt her
feelings. He didn't want to do that, now that they were

getting along again. He didn't allow himself to contemplate just how well they might get along tonight—if he pushed the right buttons. If he pushed those buttons, he could turn himself into a cinder. And then where would he be?

The charged moment passed. Penelope talked him into having a sandwich. He did, not because he was hungry, but to pass the time and to be amicable. Then, behaving as if he were dead tired, he told her he was going to bunk out on the lanai. She said she was tired, too, and she retired to the bedroom. He was relieved when he heard her lock her door.

It was only about 9:30 p.m. He hadn't gone to sleep this early since he was ten years old. He looked up at the stars, thanking God it was the last time he'd be in this situation. Tomorrow he'd be back in his own house.

He heard the waves rhythmically breaking on the rocky beach below, but he couldn't fall asleep. Pressing a button to make his watch dial light up, he checked the time. Ten o'clock. Then ten-fifteen. Ten-thirty. By eleven he'd begun to doze off, only to wake up again and again. He shifted his position and tried to make himself fall more soundly asleep.

This promised to be the longest night he'd ever live through.

Penelope turned over on the bed and glanced at her travel alarm. It was almost midnight and she still couldn't sleep. *You're a friend of my dad's. It was stupid.* Craig's words kept repeating in her mind. Why did the fact that she was a friend of Jasper's bother him particularly? From what she understood of their relationship, they hardly ever saw each other. Unless he was afraid she'd go home and tell tales. He'd once joked about that regarding his mother. But did he really think that if they made love, she'd run and tell his parents about it? And if he didn't get along with his dad, why would he care what Jasper thought, anyway? *It was stupid.* That was the thing he'd said that hurt the most. It was stupid to find her attractive?

"Oh, who knew what he meant!" she murmured to herself. If she kept on this way, she'd never fall asleep. She wanted to look alert and well-rested in the morning when she saw him, not haggard with circles under her eyes, as if she'd pined away for him all night. What would happen in the morning? she wondered, biting her fingernail. Was that the last time she would ever see him? Should she be bold and offer to take him out to dinner again?

Now why would she want to do that? she asked herself. She shouldn't *want* to see him again. How often did she have to remind herself that he was exactly the sort of man she should run from, not finagle a way to keep up an acquaintance with, like some little beggar, hoping he'd throw breadcrumbs her way again. Where was her pride? Where was her common sense? She was above this sort of behavior—and this sort of man!

She threw the sheet aside and got out of bed. Drink some milk, she told herself. Maybe a dose of calcium and tryptophan would help her get to sleep. After quietly opening the door, she tiptoed barefoot into the kitchen. The double doors to the lanai were open and she could see Craig's feet on the lounger.

But while she was distracted gazing at what she could see of him, she bumped into a kitchen chair. It scraped on the tiled floor. Darn! she thought. She hurried to the refrigerator, hoping to get the milk before he woke up.

But before she even reached the refrigerator door, he startled her by coming into the kitchen.

"What's wrong?" he asked. "I heard a noise."

"Nothing," she said, breathless. He'd taken off his shirt and was standing in front of her barechested. "Just getting some milk." He looked masculine, formidable, and gorgeous. Her heart started pounding. Oh, God, why did she have to bump into that chair? "C-couldn't sleep."

He moved closer to her, setting his hand against the corner of the refrigerator, as if to lean against it, yet he wasn't resting any weight on it. All his energy seemed focused on her. "Are you all right? You're trembling."

"Just . . . maybe I'm cold. I had the sheet covering me in bed, and it's cooler out here with the doors open."

His eyes traveled down to her shoulders, covered only with the thin straps that held up her short cotton nightgown. She found herself breathing in raggedly when his eyes crossed her breasts. He reached out and stroked her arm. His touch was so gentle, she closed her eyes, almost ready to weep.

"No goose bumps," he said. "You feel warm."

She opened her eyes and looked at him, a sudden wave of honesty shooing away the mental warning signals that told her she was doing a foolish thing by becoming too honest. But all at once she didn't care. "Craig?"

His eyes moved back and forth over hers, as if sensing something monumental was about to come from her mouth. "Yes?"

"Y-you know on the boat . . . catamaran . . . this morning?"

"Yes."

"How I made you . . . you know . . . stop?"

"I remember."

"Well, at the time I thought I was doing the right thing. And I still think I did the right thing. But..." She stopped to breathe.

"What?"

"I... All day today, I..." She bit her lip, feeling tears of need come into her eyes. "I've wished I hadn't stopped you." She drew in a long, uneven breath. There, she'd said it.

New lights came into Craig's eyes. He took his hand off the refrigerator and brushed back her hair. "I've wished that, too." His voice was quiet, low, and tender. He kissed her forehead and she leaned forward, all but falling against him. His strong arms came around her and he held her close. "I can feel your heart beating," he said with wonder. "You really do want to make love, don't you?"

"I'm afraid so," she whispered.

"Why be afraid of it?"

"Because, it's still foolish. But," she said, looking into his eyes, "I can't seem to get a grip on myself. Usually I can, even with charmers like you. Maybe I'd be tempted, but I never gave in. I guess you're my Waterloo."

He grinned at her. "I'm not sure I follow what you're talking about. But you're so adorable, it doesn't matter." He kissed her mouth softly and playfully. "So, what exactly are you saying to me now? Spell it out for me, so we don't have any more misunderstandings."

She felt as if she couldn't breathe. "I don't think I have the strength to spell it out. I'm too...embarrassed to say the words out loud."

"You weren't afraid to spell it out on the catamaran. What did you say? 'I was just supposed to look you up, not have sex with you!' Something like that."

"I'm good at saying no. It's yes I have trouble with," she explained. "Force of habit."

"Shall I spell it out, then?" he asked. "Just to be sure we're seeing eye-to-eye?"

She nodded, holding her breath.

"You're willing to sleep with me now?"

"Yes," she whispered.

"You're sure?"

She caught her lip between her teeth, not knowing how to answer. No, she wasn't sure. She knew she shouldn't be doing this....

At her hesitation, Craig set his hand on her shoulder, making her close her eyes at his warmth. "I want you to be sure," he said, slowly pushing the strap off her shoulder. She felt it slide along her arm. His hand moved downward until it pushed aside the cotton material covering her breast. He squeezed her flesh gently, then teased her nipple with his thumb. "Is this what you want?"

"Oh, Craig," she said in a sensuous sigh, leaning her forehead against his chin. "I'll die if you don't make love to me. Don't stop this time. Don't stop."

He inhaled raggedly. "That's spelling it out," he said with a surprised chuckle. He nibbled her ear and kissed her neck. "I promise I won't stop. I've been thinking about you all day, too."

"You have?" she said with a feeling of reassurance.

"I've spent more time in one day thinking about you than I've ever spent thinking about any woman. More than all of them put together. For a starched needle-pointer from Chicago, you've really done a number on me."

She smiled. "I have?"

"I couldn't stop wondering what it would be like to sleep with you. Would you be shy? Or playful and sexy?

Maybe even steamy and out of control, like an erupting volcano. My imagination's been having a field day.''

Penelope looked away in embarrassment. ''I can't even predict how I'll feel.'' She gazed at him again, growing increasingly nervous. ''I hope you won't be disappointed. I told you, I'm not very experienced.''

''Shh. Shh.'' He kissed her warmly. ''Just be yourself. Don't worry about it.'' He pushed the other strap down and caressed her breasts with such tenderness that she closed her eyes and whimpered with yearning. When he spoke, his voice was shaky with his uneven breathing. ''I have the feeling you're going to be the sweetest, sexiest lover in the world. And I'm not going to be able to get enough of you.''

She smiled and slid her arms around his neck. Nuzzling his chin with her nose, she whispered, ''I'm afraid that's how I'll feel about you. But I don't care. Right now, I just need you in my life more than I've ever needed anyone.''

He began to kiss her ardently, stroking her breast with the palm of his hand. Soon he slid his hand downward and, lifting the nightgown that still clung to her hips, he slipped his hand between her thighs. She was already slick and he quickly found her most sensitive point. She gasped as a sharp burning pleasure spiraled through her.

When she writhed against him, he kissed her even more aggressively. ''You're so aroused, so excited,'' he said as he continued to touch her below in such an expert way that she had to keep herself from crying out. Just as she thought her brain was going to go liquid with her heightening lust, he stopped.

''You know,'' he said, his voice husky, taking his hand away, ''you were right about one thing this morning. You could get pregnant. I don't have anything with me—''

Her mind suddenly focussed. "It's okay," she said, glad he remembered. "I bought some." She turned from him and reached down into the wastebasket, then showed him the box. "See?"

His eyes were alight with relief and amazement. "You bought condoms? When? Today?"

"Yes. One of those impulse purchases," she said with an impish smile. "I still had hope."

"Then what were they doing in the wastebasket?"

"I lost hope," she said, pouting as she ran her hand up his chest to his nipple. "You just don't know how many highs and lows you put me through today."

"I know. I went through them all, too. So," he said, smiling as he tore the cellophane off the box and took out a few square packets, "looks like we're all taken care of." He kissed her again, forcefully, the promise of torrid fulfillment in his lips. "Ready?"

"My knees feel weak."

"Mine, too," he said, yet he bent and slid his arm beneath her legs and lifted her up.

"You're going to carry me to bed?" she said, slipping her arms around his neck. "You're romantic, too! You're just too good to be true."

He took her into the bedroom and set her down on the sheets. Quickly he unzipped and tugged off his jeans. When she saw his taut arousal, she grew light-headed for a moment. Maybe she wasn't ready for this after all. As if in a huge hurry, he ripped open a condom package. When he'd applied the sheath, he knelt beside the bed for a moment and kissed her breasts and abdomen, even her belly button, as if worshipping her body, until her breathing grew shallow and her skin quivered. He pulled the nightgown down her legs and threw it aside. When she knew she was naked, she instinctively crossed one thigh over the other to hide herself. She saw him smile at her attempt at modesty.

Running his hand along her side, he climbed onto the bed to lie next to her. "You're a beautiful woman, Penelope. A sculpture of Venus, only warm and soft. And supple," he said, finding her breast again, feeling its contours, testing her firm flesh with his fingertips. He found her nipple and teased it until, wanting more than teasing, she snuggled closer to his male body. At her hint, he slid his arms around her and clasped her to him, his legs tangling with hers. She felt his hardness against her thigh, but had no time to grow anxious. With a sense of eagerness, he pressed her into the pillow with a tender but increasingly urgent kiss. She kissed him back fully, inhaling deeply through her nose, feeling her chest pressing into his. They began to explore and caress one another until soon their bodies were writhing in a more and more insistent rhythm.

Instinctively she allowed him between her legs, raising her knees up. He moved in such a way that his male length came against her feminine point of arousal, nudging it until she groaned with helpless desire. Just when she thought she would lose her mind, he entered her slowly, surely, making her gasp with joy. She slid her hands to his firm buttocks and pressed him closer.

He began long, forceful thrusts. Tilting her head back, she arched her neck as new sensations radiated through her body. His lips and hands and his sweetly intruding flesh brought her to an even higher erotic plateau, a state of supersensitivity she'd never felt before. Time and place faded, and her whole being centered on her body's overwhelming cry for satiation. She grew drunk on the promise of supreme fulfillment she felt with each thrust, her body rocking in a driving rhythm with his. She heard him groan while she breathed audibly with carnal craving. This was a sexual encounter far beyond her limited experience. This was so overwhelming, it began to frighten her a bit.

Craig kissed her neck as if to devour her. "You are the sexiest woman," he murmured. "You turn me on so much—I wish we could go on forever."

He withdrew almost his full length and thrust forcefully until she called out his name in agonized frustration.

He paused and raised his head to look at her face. "Am I too rough?"

"No," she said, the word more a sensual sigh. "I like it. But I didn't know it was supposed to be *this* overpowering. It scares me. Don't stop. Do it again...please..."

"You're so sweet," he whispered tenderly. "Don't be afraid of it. Let it happen," he said as he slowly moved again. The brief respite seemed to heighten her body's sensitivity to his lovemaking. She began to pant until the deep tension inside her suddenly reached a new transition, a brief state of blissful suspension. A thrilled high gasp escaped her, and then her body exploded into voluptuous convulsions. As she cried out his name, he gripped her tightly and she felt his body tense. She smiled when she felt him throbbing inside her and heard his groan of satisfaction.

As if physically spent, he lay still on top of her for a few relaxing, sublimely intimate minutes. She held him warmly in her arms as tears of contentment streamed back from her eyes and into her hair. His breathing gradually grew normal again. Carefully he rose up and moved off of her to lie beside her, pulling her against him, his head next to hers on the pillow.

"That was . . . astonishing," he said, as if at a loss for words. He stroked her arm. "You do something to me. I've never felt so close. This . . ." He laughed unsteadily. "This is strange."

"I know," she said, leaning her head against his, keeping her eyes on the ceiling, feeling a little helpless. "You're such an incredible lover," she said in a small, awed voice. She thought of her one previous attempt at a sexual relationship. That experience had been awkward and completely unfulfilling for her. But Craig had awakened her—she felt as if she'd been a virgin until now. She tried to laugh and make it all amusing in her mind, but she couldn't. "You know you've spoiled me for anyone else," she told him with a sincerity tinged by sadness.

He slid his hand down her arm and squeezed her hand, as if he understood, even resonated with what she'd told him. She heard him take in a breath as if he were going to say something. But then, he didn't.

She closed her eyes and tried not to think about anything, tried to continue to savor these beautiful moments with him. Who knew if she'd experience anything like this ever again?

Craig held Penelope in his arms, feeling his body going pleasurably limp from the powerful climax she'd given him. He'd never felt such impetuous lust or such heavenly appeasement in his life. The sensations had been so strong that, even now that it was all over, he still didn't feel like letting go of her. Instead of being sleepy from satiation, he felt wide awake and full of life, his body vibrating with a marvelous feeling of well-being. He'd never felt like this after sex before.

Of course, it had been a while. Had abstinence made the experience more enduring? If so, he ought to play the hermit more. But he had a gut feeling that wasn't the reason. He harbored a suspicion that it had something to do with Penelope—her stop-go behavior that had left him desiring her all afternoon, and then her lovely shyness tonight when she'd told him she wanted him after all. He needed to explore this relationship further. At least, he was terribly certain he wanted to experience another exquisite sexual odyssey with her. She was too exciting to walk away from. And she would be here for two whole weeks....

"I have an idea...a suggestion," he said, after mulling it over in his mind another minute.

She turned her head toward him on the pillow, and he shifted his head backward so he could see her, though the light was dim.

"What?" she asked, her moist eyes gleaming in the moonlight from the window.

"I mentioned I'll be living at that big house?"

"Yes?"

"Why don't you stay there with me—until your vacation's over, if you want."

"You mean, like...live with you?"

Her interpretation startled him a bit. "I don't know if you'd call less than two weeks living together. You can just...share my space while you're here. Put it that way."

"W-why?"

He smiled. "Why do you think? We've discovered something really extraordinary here. I want to spend more time with you...explore all the parameters of what just blossomed between us. Do you want it to end yet?"

She reached out to stroke his cheek, and he closed his eyes at the sweetness in her touch. "No, of course I don't."

He took her hand and kissed her palm. "Then stay with me," he urged.

"But . . . what happens when my vacation's over?"

Craig didn't like the question. Women always had a tendency to think ahead too much, to get to the bottom line. "Whatever happens then will happen. In the meantime, we have a dozen days and a dozen nights to spend together."

After a moment she nodded, as if some new thought had come into her mind that had convinced her. With a little smile, she said, "What we feel now is too intense not to cool down. But it would be good to let it play itself out." She paused. "I'll . . . share your space." She leaned in to kiss him affectionately on the mouth. "This will be the most memorable vacation I'll ever have."

"Good," he told her, giving her an extra kiss at the corner of her mouth. "We'll move your things over there tomorrow." They snuggled together again. She murmured she felt sleepy now, and he told her he did, too. But as she dozed off, he lay wide awake. What she'd just told him showed common sense, even a touch of unexpected sophistication, and it ought to have reassured him. But instead, her reasons for coming to his place nagged at him. Why did she assume so sensibly that they'd cool down? Obviously, every relationship did. Instead of being carried away with excitement over their new love affair, as he was, why was she already anticipating an anticlimactic ending? *It would be good to let it play itself out,* she'd said. Craig found her words damned unsettling. But when he asked himself why it unsettled him, he didn't have an answer. And that bothered him even more.

After a quarter of an hour or so mulling it all over, he decided he was intellectualizing everything too much. This was a sudden, wildly passionate relationship with an amazingly sensual woman. Trying to analyze it would defeat his purpose, which was to live it, enjoy it, however long it lasted. He'd never been one to worry about anything. Why start now?

7

The next morning when Penelope woke up in bed with Craig, she wasn't startled, but felt beautifully warm and comfortable. Already awake, he studied her with appreciative eyes. She was naked with no sheet thrown over her, yet she wasn't the least bit embarrassed, which surprised her. Craig had brought out a whole new, uninhibited part of her personality she hadn't known she possessed. She loved it and had the intuitive feeling that this was her true self, not that cautious, unexciting other self she'd been back in Chicago.

"'Morning," he said, smiling at her with a contented gleam in his eye.

She was glad he appeared to have no regrets about last night. "'Morning," she replied. "Sleep good?"

"The best."

"Me, too."

They kissed. "We're going to wake up feeling sublime every morning," he said.

"We are?"

"You're staying with me the rest of your vacation. You agreed last night." He kissed her again. "Haven't changed your mind, have you?"

"No," she replied, happy he was so anxious to keep their new relationship going. She remembered her old idea that she should avoid a man like Craig, but after last night, she realized she'd lived in the slow lane too long. She needed some excitement in her dull life. So long as they both knew where they stood, what harm was there in having a wild fling in a tropical paradise?

He ran his forefinger down her abdomen, stopping at her belly button, which he playfully poked. "I have some things to take care of today, but I'll come back this evening around six. We'll have dinner someplace in town and then I'll take you to the house where I'll be staying. Can you have your clothes packed?"

"Sure," she said. She was curious about what he had to do all day, but didn't ask. In a way, she didn't want to know. If she was going to spend the next dozen days and nights living out a sensual fantasy with a sexy man as her private pleasure guide, the less she knew about details, the better, she decided. The knowledge of his whereabouts would bring them back to reality too soon. She circled his belly button with her fingertips. "You don't have to go yet, do you?" Her hand trailed down to his manhood, swelling beneath her touch.

"You've turned into a sex kitten overnight," he said with a pleased laugh, grabbing her mischievous hand.

"Your fault," she murmured with a little pout. "You made me like it too much."

He brought her hand to his mouth and kissed it. "I do have to go, sweetheart. Sorry, but we woke up late, and I have to be someplace. Tonight we'll have our fill. It'll be beautiful."

As if to prevent her from giving him any further temptation, he kissed her mouth soundly but briefly and got out of bed. While he showered, she found her discarded nightgown and put it on, then made toast, eggs, and coffee for breakfast. When he came out dressed and clean shaven, he smiled when he saw the table set and Penelope dishing up scrambled eggs.

"Thanks!" he said, sitting down. He ate fast and with gusto.

Before she'd finished her plate, he got up and squatted next to her chair, one knee on the floor. Sliding his arms around her middle, he hugged her and kissed her neck. "After today," he promised, "no more interruptions. God, I wish I could make love with you now. Tonight, we'll jump into bed and stay there for days—and I bet we still won't have enough of each other." He laughed. "What's happening between us?"

Penelope felt flattered and excited at the way he was all but worshipping her. No man had ever wanted her this way, had ever expressed so much desire for her. "It's you," she said, running her hands through his hair. "I've blossomed just for you—that's what's so special."

His eyes took on a whole new light. "What we've discovered *is* special," he whispered. "I've never been addicted to anything, but I feel as though I'm already addicted to you." He kissed her again, warmly, and she responded from the heart. "Damn," he said, pulling away with clear reluctance. "I have to go. When I come back at six, we'll pick up where we left off and never stop. Okay?"

"Okay." She smiled as he got up to go. He squeezed her hand and then he was out the door. As she sat alone at the kitchen table, she closed her eyes, feeling her feelings, thrilled to have such an exciting man in her life.

But a new thought intruded and she opened her eyes. Craig wouldn't be in her life for long, she reminded herself. *We'll pick up where we left off and never stop.* She recalled his words and felt a certain regret, though she wished she could ignore the feeling. They *would* stop.

Their fantastic fling would end. He knew that. As she thought about it, she found it odd that he'd even said the words. He was a fantasy-spinner, full of the sort of blarney women liked to hear—a lot like her dad. Too bad, she thought with a sigh. Why was it that smooth-talking men so seldom had a smooth life?

Ah, well. Soon enough she'd be flying home to her sensible old surroundings. In the meantime, she meant to experience every nuance of the sensual fantasy Craig had begun to spin for her alone.

As Craig arrived late at his staff meeting that morning, he could barely think straight. Penelope was on his mind, her feminine voice, her exquisite body, her whole aura and being. Because of his meeting, he'd had to leave her abruptly, yet he'd wanted her so much he could still taste her mouth and smell her hair. He couldn't remember ever being so enraptured by a woman—and so suddenly. That kiss on his catamaran had been his downfall, but he hoped he'd keep on falling, it felt so marvelous.

"Sorry I'm late," he apologized to his employees, who sat around the meeting table studying him with questioning eyes. He was known for his promptness. "I got sidetracked with something important."

Ned sat at the other end of the table, the only one with a knowing smile playing around his mouth. Craig avoided eye contact with him.

"Let's begin with the revised tour schedules," Craig said, spreading out papers he'd taken off his desk on his way in. He tried to sound knowledgeable and in charge, and he soon got his head together enough to behave like the successful businessman he was.

Toward the end of the two-hour meeting, he told his staff, "By the way, I'm taking some time off. I've never given myself a vacation." He smiled. "I used to think my whole life was a vacation."

His employees laughed.

"But I feel like I need some time away from the job. At least a week, maybe more. I'll spend the afternoon getting things in order, making arrangements for some of you to take over my duties where needed. I'll be back at the beginning of August for the usual tourist frenzy. Any questions?"

Everyone looked surprised, but no one said anything. Across the table, however, Ned's eyes were bright with humor. When he opened his mouth to speak, Craig stood and said with finality, "Meeting's adjourned."

Afterward, Ned stopped by Craig's office. "Your floors are drying nicely. Checked them before coming here. I'll get one of the guys to help me move your bed back into place, since you're busy today."

"Thanks, I appreciate it."

Ned eyed him, looking smug with secret knowledge. Craig braced himself for his friend's inevitable teasing.

"It's that pretty wahine, isn't it? The one Sophie saw you with."

"I'm just taking a well-deserved vacation, that's all."

"By yourself?"

"No."

"Didn't think so. Where?"

"That's a secret," Craig said with impatience. "Even from you."

"But what if there's some emergency and we need to reach you?"

"I'll phone in every day and check."

"If you're spending your vacation in bed, you might forget."

Craig closed his eyes, annoyed with the truth in his needling admonition. He leaned against the window frame and turned to Ned. "All right, I'll tell you, but you're not to tell anyone else where I can be reached. I don't want to be bothered, except for a real emergency, understand?"

"Got it. So, where will you be?"

"Home."

"Aha! With the new lady Sophie's sure you're falling for?"

Craig blinked. "Falling for? I'm not . . . it's just a . . . a physical attraction. She's only here for a couple of weeks. Sure, we've got a hot thing going, and while it's going, I want to experience it to the fullest. I want to . . . be my old self again, have back my life from the old days when I had plenty of time to enjoy a woman's company."

Ned was listening, but shaking his head.

"What?" Craig asked.

"You're going backward, boss. You're in transition, but you need to move forward, not back to the old days. I told you, you're not in your twenties anymore."

"So what?"

Ned scratched his nose, but didn't answer. "What about this lady? She's just letting you show her a good time on her vacation?"

"Yeah," Craig replied, sounding argumentative.

His old friend exhaled slowly, as if disappointed. "So she's just another chick from the mainland, looking for a cozy fling in Hawaii before she goes back home to her boyfriend?"

"She doesn't have a boyfriend."

"Oh." Ned looked more hopeful now. "But she's got the hots for you?"

Craig rolled his eyes. "It appears that way."

"So you're just going along for the ride? Why pass up a good thing—is that it?"

"It's not like that. She's different. She's . . . special," he said, remembering the word she'd used earlier.

"Different. Special." Ned seemed to enjoy repeating Craig's description. "But you're not falling for her, like Sophie thought."

"No way! I'm not that dumb. You think I want to wind up at some church altar? Get real!"

Ned chuckled as he headed for the door. "Boss, one of these days, maybe *you're* going to 'get real'!"

What in blazes was *that* supposed to mean? Craig wondered as Ned walked out. He grabbed a newspaper on his desk and threw it into the wastebasket in impatient annoyance. The hell with it, he thought, putting Ned's comment out of his mind. He had a full afternoon of work to do, so he could leave this damned office behind for a while and enjoy an exquisite interlude with Penelope.

Her bags packed and waiting, Penelope put down the needlepoint piece she was stitching, a Medieval lady with a unicorn, and checked her watch again. It was six-twenty. Craig was late. Had he changed his mind? As she began to bite her fingernail, she heard the key turn in the door. All at once he burst in.

"Hi, sweetheart." He took her in his arms as she got up from her chair. "Sorry. Had too many things to take care of."

"Is everything okay?" she asked worriedly.

"Everything's copacetic," he said with a broad smile. "I've got nothing but time on my hands now—to spend with you."

She grinned with relief. His arms around her tightened and he kissed her thoroughly. When his mouth left hers, she felt giddy with happiness. "I'm so glad," she told him. "I've been looking forward to seeing you all day. I got nervous when six o'clock came and went, afraid you'd had second thoughts."

"No second thoughts. Not a one."

"Me, either."

"Great. Let's go!" He picked up her bags and they left.

As they walked through the parking lot, he carried her luggage to a new-looking Porsche sports car instead of to her rental car. When he opened the trunk to load the bags, she asked, "Whose car is this?"

The question seemed to take him by surprise. "Well . . . it comes with the house I'm taking care of. I take care of the car, too."

"Oh. Gosh, it's beautiful. Leather seats and everything," she said, peeking in the window as he closed the trunk.

"Get in," he said, opening the door for her.

She did, and he got behind the wheel. He started the car, revving the motor a bit, as if to impress her.

"Sounds . . . copacetic," she said.

He looked at her in a puzzled way. "What?"

"Isn't that the word you used before? Copacetic?"

"Yes, but that's not quite the correct usage. It means 'entirely satisfactory.' It's usually used to describe how things are going, how life's treating you, that sort of meaning."

"I see. I'm not sure I've ever heard it before."

"It's my favorite word, even if it *is* educated slang."

She laughed as he drove the car onto the road to town. They ate dinner at an Italian restaurant, where, again, the

proprietor and many of the waiters knew Craig. Here
their dinner was not half price—it was on the house. Penelope was mystified, but decided not to ask questions.

Afterward, he drove her some distance up the coast,
turning onto a road that led through the steep hills high
above a black rock beach Craig said was called Napoopoo. Soon he turned onto a narrow one-lane road that led
through thick foliage, eventually arriving at a large, two-
story house with white pillars and a well-kept lawn and
garden.

"Is this the place?" she asked with astonishment. "It's
so beautiful."

Craig smiled and almost looked as though he was
about to say *thanks*. Instead he said, "Come on in. I'll
show you around."

He unlocked the front door and they walked into a
large living room empty of furniture, except for a couch.
Penelope couldn't help but be impressed with the beautiful wood floor that shone with a rich luster. In one corner, a grand, curved staircase led upstairs. One wall of the
room featured floor-to-ceiling windows that overlooked
the bay and the ocean.

"Gosh, this is impressive. The view is gorgeous.
Beautiful wood, too," she said, looking down. "I hate to
step on it."

Craig bent to touch the floor with his fingertips. "It's
dry—just been refinished. Upstairs, too. That's why I
couldn't stay here last night."

"I see. Where are the owners?"

Craig stood again, rubbing his fingertips with his
thumb. "I'm not sure."

"Is this a vacation home?"

"Sort of. As you can see, there's not much furniture
yet. Enough for me, though."

"So you'll be staying here, taking care of the place, whenever they're gone?"

"Yes."

"Where do you go when they do come in?"

He shrugged. "I'll figure that out when the time comes. It's not a problem."

Penelope felt sad for him. She wished he could develop more of a need for stability and permanency in his life. But if he did, she supposed he'd become another boring pillar of society.

"This used to be the home of a coffee grower," he told her. "But he and his family built a new home inland, closer to the coffee groves, when the traffic began to increase and it got to be a chore to drive home to the coast. He held on to this house, hoping one of his children would want it, but, strangely, none of them did. So he finally sold it."

"When did the sale take place?"

"About four months ago."

"Have you stayed here before, or have the new owners been using it?"

"I've . . . been here before," he answered quickly. He grabbed her hand. "Come on, I'll show you the view from the master bedroom upstairs."

"Sure," she said, following him up the spectacular wood staircase. She sensed she'd been asking him too many questions and instructed herself not to pry any more. They were here for fun—no use spoiling things by making him uncomfortable.

He led her down the second-floor hallway to a large bedroom furnished with a mahogany dresser and a king-size bed. This room looked the most lived-in and even had a decorative Oriental carpet on the shining wood floor. He took her through the room to the French doors, which he opened. They stepped outside onto the lanai, larger than the one at Jasper's condo. There were some newly painted white wrought-iron chairs and a small table on the balcony. She walked past them to the decorative iron railing.

"The view from up here is even better," she said. "I can see more of the little beach."

"I know. The sunsets are fantastic. You'll see in a half hour or so."

She turned to him and slipped her arms around his waist. "What'll we do until then?"

He slid his hands up her back. "I don't know. Got any ideas?"

"Is that the bed where you sleep?" she asked, glancing at the big bed inside.

"That's the bed where *we'll* sleep."

"Maybe I should try it out, just to make sure it suits me."

He grinned and gave her a squeeze. "I think you should."

Eagerly—too eagerly, she knew, but she didn't see any reason to be coy—she headed for the bed, with Craig right behind her. She stretched out on the quilt bedspread and smiled up at him.

"Suits me perfectly," she said, her voice growing languid. She'd been thinking about being in bed with him again all day long.

He gazed up and down the length of her and, his eyes brightening with desire, murmured, "You look like you were born for this bed." He began to climb over her, sliding his body alongside hers. "*You* suit *me* perfectly. This is better than I imagined it would be—and I've been distracted daydreaming about you all day."

She grew breathless with anticipation. "Guess we can stop fantasizing about it and actually do—" She gasped and forgot what she was saying as he pushed down her flowered tank top and fondled her breast, his thumb quickly finding her nipple.

Propped up on his elbow, he looked down at her with appreciative eyes. "No bra," he said.

"I felt sexier leaving it off," she said in a whispery voice. "It makes it easier—" she closed her eyes as he began to fondle her other breast "—for you to touch me."

"You respond so sweetly," he murmured, observing her facial expressions as he caressed her.

She made an erotic little whimper. "You have such wonderful hands. Do more to me...."

"Happy to," he said, grabbing hold of her upper arm as he slid over her, moving closer to her face. He kissed her mouth, his lips moving hotly against hers. She felt a new, more torrid flame of desire ignite between them. Her hips began to undulate beneath him as her pent-up need for him took over her psyche. When his mouth moved from her lips, down her throat, she arched her head back and murmured urgently, "Craig, don't tease me too much. I'm ready. Take off my clothes."

But instead his mouth fastened onto her nipple, driving her wild with an even more intense sensation. "You're heartless!" she breathed, writhing with spiraling need. "I've waited all day. Don't make me wait now."

His chuckle was low and sexy as he lifted his head from her swelling breast. "I couldn't if I wanted to." He unbuttoned her shorts and pulled them down, along with her panties. She lifted her hips to make their removal easier. Anxious to be naked, she pulled her tank top over her head. She unbuttoned his cotton shirt while he unfastened his belt and pulled down his zipper. As he removed his clothes, she smiled with anticipation when she saw his taut arousal.

Her heart rate accelerating, she reached for her purse, which she'd tossed on the bed earlier. She found the box of condoms she'd remembered to bring along, but fumbled opening it because her fingers were shaking. He took out a small square packet, extracted the sheath and applied it.

She parted her thighs as he moved over her again. When he paused to stroke her most sensitive spot, already moist, she moaned. "Craig...please..."

He shifted his position and the instant she felt his hardness nudging her there, she used her hand to guide him quickly inside her.

"You feel so good," he murmured, kissing her mouth. "You turn me to fire."

Penelope felt dazed with pleasure experiencing his hard masculinity again. "You make me feel so sexy—I just lose all control with you." As he began rocking motions with his pelvis, she slid her hands to his buttocks. He kissed her throat, breathing heavily now, his body tensing in her arms with each manly thrust. Penelope closed her eyes in a delirium of racing need. Yet she tried to keep her wits about her, difficult as it was. She wanted to remember every single second of their intimacy, for she would have to live on these sublime moments, on the memory of Craig's lovemaking, for a long, long time.

They missed the sunset. But it didn't matter. Soon they made love all over again in the dark, the ocean breeze from the open French doors cooling their heated bodies.

The next few days passed languidly and erotically. They barely left the bedroom. Once, in the moonlight, and another time in the morning sun, they made love on the lanai. Penelope thought surely they'd get tired of making love so much, but it didn't happen. She began to wonder how she'd ever learn to live without sex again—without Craig—once she got back home. But, like Scarlett O'Hara, she decided to worry about that tomorrow.

In between lovemaking, they talked a lot. She began to like that part of their temporary relationship as much as the sex. She told him about her loneliness as an only child, about her irresponsible father and her parents' unhappy marriage. He described what it was like growing up as Jasper's son and explained why he'd exiled himself from his family. Sometimes they laughed about favorite old movies or argued about what toppings were best on a pizza.

One day, when they went down to the kitchen to make sandwiches for lunch—Craig seemed to have stocked the refrigerator—he asked her how she'd decorate the living room and dining room, if the house were hers.

She walked through the rooms wearing nothing but one of his shirts and let her imagination run wild. Traditional European furniture, she told him, with touches of the East—more Oriental rugs, such as the one in the bedroom, only bigger and more elaborate. On the walls she'd put large needlepoint tapestries, perhaps depicting Hawaiian flora and fauna. "I'd make it look rich and ornate," she said. "Though the tapestries would take forever to stitch."

"How long?" he asked with apparent genuine interest.

She chuckled. "Probably a lifetime to finish as many as you'd need for this room."

He lowered his eyes and seemed to look almost sad for a moment. Perhaps she only imagined it. When he looked up at her, he smiled and said, "Sounds fabulous."

"It's always fun to imagine," she said. "I wonder how the owners will decorate it."

Craig exhaled. "God only knows." His tone was curiously ironic.

After three cozy days indoors, Craig took her to see the volcanoes in the national park on the southern portion of the island. Penelope surprised him by readily agreeing when he suggested they take a helicopter over the lava flows. They spent a spectacular day together. She wore the revealing black tank top she'd bought and enjoyed the womanly satisfaction of easily drawing Craig's attention away from the red-hot volcano. She constantly caught him studying her with smoldering admiration in his eyes.

The next day he drove her down to Napoopoo Beach to snorkel in the bay's underwater sea-life sanctuary. This time she used only a life jacket, which allowed her to move about with him more freely, and she got used to the mask and snorkel. They spent several glorious hours together. As they drove back to the house in the late afternoon, it began to rain.

He parked the Porsche and they got out. Instead of heading for the house, she began walking through the grounds of the mansion. Craig followed. Both were still wearing their bathing suits.

"Where are you going?" he asked, slipping his arm around her as he caught up with her near a border of neatly trimmed and blooming red hibiscus.

"I haven't gotten out here yet to look at the flowers," she said.

He chuckled. "But it's raining. Weren't you the girl that didn't like to get wet?"

She gave him a playful shove. "We're still in our bathing suits, so what difference does it make?"

"You sure have changed," he said, giving her a squeeze. "Are you going to revert to your old self when you go back to Chicago?"

Penelope wiped rain from her face and didn't answer, not knowing how to respond. She didn't like to think about going back. "The rains here are so nice," she said, looking up at the clouded sky. "Warm and soft."

"Like you," he said, nuzzling the side of her face with his nose.

Without even thinking about it, she inclined herself against his body. She'd grown so used to being near him, it felt like the most natural thing she'd ever done.

He took her in his arms, and they kissed. Their wet bodies grew heated as their kiss deepened. She felt a tug on the tie of her bikini top at the back of her neck. Then he unfastened the back clasp.

She smiled with delight. "Can anyone see us here?" she asked, her breaths coming faster, no longer surprised at how quickly sweet lust flamed between them.

"The house is surrounded by lots of property and lots of foliage. No one can see."

Her top dropped to the grass at her feet. His eyes ignited with desire as he brought his hands up to caress her. His masculine fingers slid over her soft mounds of flesh, slippery from the rain. The drops of cool water washing over her gave her an exquisitely erotic feeling, making her skin and her nipples ultrasensitive to the heat of his touch.

"Craig, Craig," she whispered, leaning her forehead against his chin as he continued to arouse her. When she'd grown so exquisitely tormented it seemed she could no longer focus her eyes, his hands slipped around her back and he pulled her to him tightly. He ardently kissed her neck and shoulder while his hands glided over her moistened skin.

"You're even more beautiful when you're wet," he murmured against her throat.

Penelope could barely stand the tension rising in her body. "I'm wet...everywhere," she whispered, her voice quivering with aching need. "Take me to bed."

As if growing agitated with need himself, he looked around, then led her to a small, round, wrought-iron garden table with two chairs, similar to the ones on the lanai. It was surrounded on three sides by brightly flowering hibiscus bushes. After pulling off his swimming trunks, he tugged down her bikini bottom and she stepped out of it.

"Here?" she asked, her heart beating at an increasingly elevated pace. She laughed with surprise as he sat down and pulled her toward him. Sitting astride him, facing him, she said, "I've never been naked outdoors before. In the rain. And with a man."

"A new adventure," he said, then kissed her.

"You've made my whole life one big adventure," she told him as he pulled her forward and suckled her breast. His hand reached between her parted thighs. The acute sensation brought tears to her eyes and she lifted her hands to his hair to press his face into her chest. "I love the way you make love to me, Craig. I love what you do to me."

"It's what you do to *me*," he breathed, lifting his head to kiss her fiercely on the mouth. His hands slid to her buttocks, pulling her toward his taut maleness.

Her eager fingers guided him inside her. The comforting sensation of being filled with him brought new tears. "You're a part of me, now." She closed her eyes. "No one else will ever make me feel the way you do. No one..."

He raised his hips to thrust, his hands at her buttocks pushing her against him sensually. She gasped at the erotic feeling and began to use her thigh muscles to move back and forth rhythmically. As they writhed together in unbridled ecstasy, she arched her neck backward, throwing her chest forward. She closed her eyes again in rapture, feeling his mouth working hotly at her breasts while his manhood pulsed inside her. He moaned as he climaxed, pressing the side of his face against her soft flesh.

She felt her own moment of fulfillment coming and she wrapped her arms around his head and shoulders. She began to breathe in gasps that soon turned to sobs. Hot tears streamed from her eyes, flowing with the rain down her face. "Craig!" she exclaimed. "I love you. I love you. I love you—" She cried out as she fell deliriously into torrid spasms of deep satiation. When her body quieted, she still held him close, not wanting him to let go. "I love you so much," she whispered into his wet hair.

And then she realized what she'd said. She noticed that he'd grown very still in her embrace. Self-conscious now, she slowly pulled her arms away. He paused a moment, then lifted his head to look at her. His eyes carried an expression she'd seen before, when they'd first met—a hint of wariness, even a trace of alarm.

With both hands, she tried to wipe the rain and tears from her face. "Gosh," she said, making an effort to smile and make light of it, "I really got carried away that time."

He nodded and glanced to one side. "Great sex can do that sometimes. We'd better go in the house and dry off."

"Right, " she quickly agreed, getting up from sitting astride him. "We'd better."

They walked into the house, found towels in a downstairs bathroom, and dried off. She went upstairs to the master bathroom, showered in the tiled shower stall, and took the black tank top she'd worn the day before off a hanger over the tub. She'd rinsed it out last night so she could wear it again. With a towel around her wet hair, she walked back to the bedroom to her suitcase and found some clean panties and short shorts. She noticed Craig coming out of the bedroom closet, whose door was usually closed. She was astonished to see it was a large walk-in closet, with quite a few men's garments hanging inside—jackets, ties and shirts. He came out with a shirt and pants and closed the door. Were all those clothes his? she wondered. Or was he borrowing from clothing that the owners had left behind?

The thought upset her a bit, but she put it out of her mind. She had more important things to think about—like what she'd said at the height of passion. *I love you so much.* Oh, God, was it true? she asked herself as she heard him start the shower running in the bathroom. She was glad he was in another room, so he couldn't see her shaken state of emotion. In a moment she found herself in tears again. It was true, she had to admit to herself. She'd been avoiding thinking about her feelings for days. But she had indeed fallen in love with Craig. She'd made exactly the same mistake her mother had made. Except perhaps she had more luck than her mother—Craig would never want to marry her.

She was safe. But her heart would certainly be broken when she had to part from him. She shook her head with a feeling of hopelessness. They had about another week together. Maybe their passion would burn itself out by then. Maybe she'd get sensible again and be able to cure herself of him. *And maybe the sun wouldn't rise tomorrow,* she thought with self-inflicted sarcasm. Already she knew the truth—she'd never get over Craig.

In a few minutes he came out dressed in crisp, light-colored pants and a cotton shirt. He glanced at her with hesitation and concern. She'd hoped that he'd forgotten her outburst, but it appeared he hadn't.

He sat on the bed. "Something just occurred to me a few minutes ago," he said. "Sit down."

What was this all about? Did he want to end their relationship already because of what she'd said? She felt anxiety rising up her neck as she sat next to him on the bed, leaving a little distance between them.

"In the garden...we didn't use a condom," he told her, pausing to take a breath. "There's a chance you could get—"

"Oh, my God," she said, lifting her fingertips to her mouth in shock. "I never thought of it. I just...got carried away."

"It's my fault—I took off your top and fondled you. After that, I couldn't think of anything but... Look, if you do get...pregnant," he said, as if wishing he could avoid the word, "don't worry. I'll see that you're taken care of."

It took a moment before his words sank in. He'd take care of her? How? She looked at him questioningly. "What do you mean? Or—" Another possible interpretation came to her. "I wouldn't have an abortion, if that's what you mean."

His eyes widened. "No, I didn't mean that. I just meant that I would provide for you...and the...child."

"With what?" she couldn't help but ask. "You can barely support yourself."

She watched the changing expressions in his eyes, trying to decipher them, but unable to.

"I'll find some way," he said, sounding sure of himself. "I just don't want you to worry about it. Look, if we're lucky, you won't be pregnant and everything will be okay."

She nodded. "I hope so." She began to do some quick mental calculations. "Actually," she said in a lighter tone, "we should be safe. I think I'm well past ovulation. I'm in the premenstral phase now. Which probably explains my...my emotional reaction earlier. Women sometimes get that way. Hormones, you know." She felt grateful to have found an excuse, one that a man would believe anyway.

He listened, studying her intently. For a moment he looked quite relieved. "I understand—that is, as well as a guy can understand a woman's cycles." He blinked. "It's funny. I seem to communicate with you better than with any other female I've met. Look at the way we just talked this through." And then he rubbed his chin and seemed to grow uneasy again.

"Something wrong?" she asked.

"No," he said. "Why don't we go into town and have dinner?"

She smiled. "Sounds nice. I just need to dry my hair first."

As Craig drove along the winding roads that led to town, he didn't say much, his mind too preoccupied. The past week with Penelope had been a picnic full of bliss and then suddenly, this afternoon, everything had turned so serious. Worry about a pregnancy *was* serious—it had been stupid of him not to think of using a condom. Usually she remembered. How could they both have forgotten themselves to that extent? He'd never allowed himself to take such a chance with a woman before. What if she became pregnant with his child?

The thought ought to have made him cold with anxiety over an unwanted responsibility, but he felt more disconcerted than anxious. Perhaps even a little excited. He realized he might be harboring some unsettled feeling that his younger brothers, both of whom were already dads, had moved ahead of him in life experience. But most of all, he found himself worrying about Penelope.

His unexpected reactions confused him, just as he'd felt confused earlier in the garden when she'd exclaimed that she loved him. One or two other women had told him that over the years, and he'd only felt a regretful sympathy for them because he did not share the feeling. But when Penelope had said the words, clasping him against her soft skin, it had brought tears to his eyes. That had never happened before.

Something very unnerving was going on—they were just too sympatico. They talked things over so damned easily and got along far too well. Usually he felt a definite separation between himself and a woman. He was he, and she was she, and the only time they fused was momentarily during sex. But he'd felt some unusual connection to Penelope ever since the beginning, before they'd even had sex, and the feeling of connectedness had only grown. It was getting a little scary.

"Where will we eat?" she asked, sounding tense. He realized he'd been so wrapped up in his thoughts, he'd been ignoring her.

"Doesn't matter," he replied, making it a point to smile. "The Italian place?"

"Okay. I liked it there."

"Good," he said. But he was beginning to wish she hadn't learned to like all the things he did. She'd become too much a part of his life. Thank God she was going back to Chicago in a week!

But at that thought, Craig felt a sudden surge of panic. What the hell was the matter with him?

"This Italian restaurant looks interesting," Bea said as they walked up the street in Kailua-Kona looking for a place to have dinner. She paused to study the menu in the window. "They have all kinds of pasta dishes."

"Whatever you want," Jasper said dispiritedly. "I don't care what I eat."

They went in and a waiter showed them to a booth. Jasper didn't even have enough interest in dinner to read the menu. "You order something for me, Bea."

"Jasper, what is your problem? You're bummed just because you haven't seen Craig and Penelope anywhere lately? Maybe they're together somewhere, happy."

"But her rental car hasn't moved from its parking space for days now. And at night there's no light in her condo. Where could she be, without a car? And what happened to him?"

"Maybe they're at his home," Bea said. "Though I still have a difficult time imagining Penelope staying with a man she's just met—even if he is our handsome Craig."

"If I could just manage to find his house," Jasper muttered, annoyed with himself. He'd tried, using a map and the address the private detective had given him. "The narrow roads in those steep hills are like a maze. And everything's so overgrown, it might as well be a rain forest. The houses you *can* see don't seem to have addresses on them. I wonder how people who live in that area get their damned mail!"

"Local people know their way around. I'm glad we couldn't find Craig's place. You'd probably stake yourself out there with your binoculars and a notepad. It's unseemly for a man of your prominence to spy on anybody, even your own son."

"Maybe I should hire back that detective. He managed to find Craig's house."

"If you do, then I'm catching the next flight home!"

Jasper drew in a breath at his wife's statement. Bea rarely made threats, and she never made them idly. If she said she'd fly home, then he knew she would. "All right, all right. No detective." He picked up the menu, feigning interest. "Let's see, what looks good for dinner?"

Bea studied her own menu, apparently placated, and they were quiet for a few moments. The waiter soon came and they both ordered vegetarian pasta dishes. He took their menus and walked away. Jasper stared dully at the place setting in front of him, wondering how he could have lost the ball this way in his quest to match Craig with Penelope. His positive thinking seemed to be failing, and he didn't know why.

Then the answer hit him like a stroke of lightning. He realized he hadn't *been* thinking positively the past few days. No wonder the universe wasn't working in his favor. He mentally set about making an immediate change in his attitude.

"Oh, my goodness," Bea said quietly.

Jasper looked up. "What?"

"Promise you won't look and you'll keep calm? Penelope and Craig just walked in."

He kept himself from turning his head. "Where?"

"A waiter's showing them to a table to our left on the other side of the room."

"Quick," he said with alarm, "put on your hat and glasses, before they see us." He grabbed his from the seat next to him. "We're back in action!"

"Jasper, really," Bea said grudgingly as she began to twist her long hair into a knot.

"Hurry!"

"But I always put up my hair so the hat covers it."

"No time, Bea! Get that hat on!"

After Craig and Penelope were seated at a table, the waiter handed them menus and left. Craig tried to put all the issues churning in his mind aside. He'd feel better once he'd eaten, he told himself.

After perusing her menu, Penelope closed it, apparently having made her choice.

Craig looked over the vast array of dishes and couldn't make up his mind. "What are you having?" he asked.

"Angel hair pasta..." she said, her voice trailing off. She was looking to her right. "There's that funny couple again."

Craig followed her gaze. Penelope was right—there they were, bright shirts, straw hats and sunglasses. "I thought we'd lost them. How can they see in here with sunglasses on? It's not brightly lit." He noticed the woman's gray-white hair beneath her hat brim bunched and trailing downward between her narrow shoulders. "Wait a minute..." he said, disbelieving his own perception.

"What?"

"That looks like Mom... For God's sake, it *is* her and that's my dad! I can tell by his hands and chin."

"Really?" She turned to glance at the couple. "They are both small-sized, like your parents. Same body types. And it does look like your mom's hair under the hat."

She looked at Craig. "But why would they be here in Hawaii?"

"Checking on things, no doubt," Craig said with angry sarcasm.

"I guess they haven't seen us," Penelope said. "Let's go say hello."

"No!" Craig took his napkin from his lap and threw it on the table. "We're leaving."

"Leaving?" she said as he got up. "Why?"

"Just walk out with me now, and don't even look in their direction."

Her eyes grew troubled, but she did as he asked. When they passed the restaurant manager, Craig apologized for leaving, saying something unexpected had come up.

Quickly he took her back to the Porsche, got in and started the motor.

"What's the matter?" she asked. "Why wouldn't you say hello? I know you don't get along with your dad, but what about your mother?"

"Hopefully they didn't see us, so she won't feel bad," Craig replied, though he doubted they'd escaped his parents' notice.

"Why have they been going around dressed like that?" Penelope wondered.

"It's a disguise," Craig said. Penelope might as well know the truth. He was too angry to make things look pretty for her. "Jasper's here to spy on us. He probably dragged my mom along for the ride."

"Spy on us?" Penelope sounded as if she were about to break out in laughter.

He realized he'd have to begin at the beginning or she would never understand the machinations of Jasper's mind. As he drove back home—he'd lost his appetite and didn't know where else to go—he told her how Jasper had married off his two younger sons to women of his choice. He told her about the wedding pillows and Jasper's "needlepoint voodoo."

Penelope looked at him incredulously. "I sold him those canvases. I sell them to lots of other customers, too. There's nothing uncommon about it. I never heard of any such thing as 'needlepoint voodoo.'"

"That's because my dad invented it," Craig said with annoyance. "I don't know whether it works or not. All I do know is that both my brothers are married to the women he set them up with. I knew my turn would come soon."

"Your turn?"

"Why do you think we've been running into them so often? Dad's following us around, trying to see if his plan is working."

"What plan?"

"Can't you put two and two together?" Craig said with impatience. "He talked you into using his condo for a vacation. Why do you think he went to all that trouble for you? Just because he thought you were a deserving young woman? He asked you to look me up. Why do you think he wanted you to meet me?"

Penelope grew quiet, apparently beginning to add things up. Too angry to say any more just now, he left her to tie the pieces together in her mind. How humiliating, he thought to himself, turning off the main road to head for his house. How revolting to have a father so manipulative as to try to arrange his whole life, to plant Penelope in his path....

With a thud, Craig realized how completely he'd fallen into his father's trap. He felt thoroughly stupid now, because he'd figured it out himself within an hour of meeting Penelope. As soon as she'd told him she had a needlepoint shop and related the particulars of how Jasper had offered her his condo, he'd known what his dad's ulterior motives had been. And yet Craig had still gotten involved with her. He'd become so caught up in his unexpected desire for her, in their heated sexual relationship, that he'd basically forgotten all about Jasper and his marriage plans.

Well, Craig had never let his dad run his life in the past, and he wasn't going to give in to his manipulations now! There was no way in heaven or hell that Craig would *ever* get married, not even to Penelope.

As Penelope sat next to Craig, who seemed to be silently seething as he drove the car, she began to unravel what he'd meant. Jasper had more or less talked her into coming to the island, she had to admit. And he'd asked her to look up Craig. And it was quite odd that Jasper had flown in with Bea, had said nothing to them, yet had been appearing here and there in what she had to agree with Craig was a disguise. But why would Jasper have chosen her for his son to marry? Perhaps the millionaire thought she'd have a stabilizing effect on his unsettled eldest.

And then another, more devastating question came into her mind. Why had Craig allowed her into his life, if he knew all along that Jasper had set them up? She remembered his reaction that first night when she'd told him she ran a needlepoint shop. He must have guessed at that moment what his father was up to. Why had he started making love with her, continued to make love to her day after day, until she'd started to care for him? It just showed how irresponsible he was. It showed how foolish she'd been, when she ought to have known better from her mother's experience. Craig was even worse than her dad, who at least had had some purpose in his pursuits, however self-serving they might have been. Craig had toyed with her for the fun of it, to appease his obviously powerful sex drive. He'd never thought beyond the moment, and now that Jasper had shown up, he had the nerve to be angry that his father had *wanted* them to meet.

Their little love nest now seemed like a viper's nest. Penelope couldn't wait to get out of it.

By the time he pulled up in front of the house, Penelope was also seething with anger. She got out of the car and slammed the door.

"I'm going up to pack my things," she told him in a tight voice, "and then I'll need a cab to take me to a hotel."

He stared at her in the dimming light as the sun set, looking dumbfounded. Then he rubbed his nose and said, "All right. I suppose it's best we don't…" He didn't finish.

"Sleep together?" she taunted. "Not in the mood anymore, since Jasper's turned up?" Her voice began to shake with hostility. "You wouldn't like to take advantage of me one last time before we call it quits? We had some pretty hot sessions. Look at me, wearing this skimpy tank top, no bra, all for you! I would have thought you'd like to pull off my clothes once more for old time's sake!"

He appeared even more dumbfounded. "You're blaming our whole relationship on me? You weren't exactly uncooperative!"

"No, I was silly enough to be attracted to you," she said with self-derision. "I didn't realize you were having a laugh on your father, toying with the woman he wanted you to marry when you never intended to have *any* sort of meaningful relationship. You've played me for a fool, and I've been one!'' she exclaimed, tears filling her eyes.

"It wasn't like that," Craig said, trying to take her by the shoulders. She evaded his grasp. "I didn't intentionally take advantage of you. When I first saw you, I thought you were exactly the sort of woman I wouldn't be attracted to. But before I realized what was happening, this . . . this overpowering desire flared between us. I didn't plan it. You didn't plan it. It just happened. We got involved and I forgot all about my dad, until I saw him tonight. I feel like a fool, too.''

She didn't buy his explanation, but it was useless to argue. All she wanted was to get out of there. "I don't want to talk to you anymore. I'm packing. Call me a cab, will you?''

"I'll drive you back to the condo," he said.

"I don't want to go *there*, either! I don't want to have anything more to do with you or your father. You're both treacherous, as far as I'm concerned, and I intend to get as far away as possible from you two, as quickly as I can!''

"Let me drive you to a hotel, then," Craig offered.

"Call me a cab," she said in a voice so firm her jaws felt locked together.

He swallowed. "Where will you go?''

"None of your damned business!''

She ran into the house and up the stairs. As she threw her things into her bags, she heard Craig on the phone downstairs calling a cab. In five minutes she was packed. A cab rolled up in the driveway in ten minutes. During all this time, neither said a word to each other. She came down with her suitcases. Craig offered to help her carry them, but she refused his assistance. He followed as she walked outside toward the waiting cab.

"So, it's just going to end like this?" he asked.

She looked at him over her shoulder, but kept walking. "How do you expect it to end, under the circumstances?"

"I didn't expect it to be so ugly."

"Neither did I." She recalled how she'd tried to commit to memory every moment with him, so that she could live on her memories forever. Now she didn't want to remember any of it. He'd taken away her fantasy, too. Men like him were nothing but destructive. Her mother had warned her.

All at once she felt his hand tugging at her elbow. There were tears in her eyes now, so she didn't turn to look at him.

"Do you have my phone number? Let me give it to you."

"Why?" she said in a cold voice. "I won't have any reason to call you."

She felt his breath near her ear. "What if... what if you're pregnant?" he whispered. "We'd need to talk then."

She closed her eyes and a tear ran down her cheek. "I'm not," she assured him. "How admirable that you have a sense of responsibility. Where was it when you took 'the sort of woman you *wouldn't* be attracted to' to bed in the first place?"

He tugged on her arm with some force this time, making her turn around. "Can't we stop these recriminations and be civil to each other?" he said. He saw the tear on her cheek and wiped it away. She flinched at his touch. "I don't know why this happened," he said. "There aren't any good reasons. But I don't like to see you leave here hating me."

She straightened her posture and blinked moisture from her eyes, clearing her vision. "I don't hate you. I have no feeling toward you at all anymore. I'm numb."

"But you did—you said you loved me." His eyes grew strangely wide as he said the words. He looked almost vulnerable for a moment, and then, as if on purpose, he lowered his eyes and set his jaw. The light was dim. Maybe she'd imagined that brief, woeful look.

"I said it during sex. You ought to know something uttered in the erotic throes of passion doesn't mean much. You made me feel a lot of things—for about two minutes. Now it's all finished. The fantasy is done. I have to get back to my real life. So should you—whatever sort of real life you have." She bit her lip. "Goodbye, Craig. It's been . . . an experience."

She turned and hurried toward the cab. The driver had gotten out and he took her luggage, loading it into the trunk. She slid into the back seat and closed the door. The cab windows were open. While the driver took his seat behind the wheel, Craig rushed up to her window.

"Don't go yet," he said, his voice full of urgency.

"Why not?" She was growing unnerved by his attempts to hang on, unable to find a reason for such desperate behavior on his part.

"I think we ought to talk more," he insisted. "There's more we need to say."

"Like what?"

His eyes shifted back and forth. "I don't know exactly," he blurted. "But we shouldn't leave each other before we figure out what we need to say!"

She shook her head. "You've lost your marbles. What could we possibly have to talk about? It's over. There *is* no more. You'll find someone new by tomorrow night, if not sooner. It won't even have to be someone new—

you seem to know all the women in town." She turned to the cabdriver. "Would you start driving, please? Now!"

The driver began to back up to turn around on the broad driveway.

"I don't want anyone else!" Craig exclaimed, keeping up with the moving cab, his hands grasping the window frame.

Penelope stared at him, wondering why he was saying such a thing after being so angry about his dad's attempt to pair them together. She wondered if he realized he was contradicting himself. This was a new aspect of him she'd never seen—he was schizophrenic!

"Let go of the cab," she told him, "or you'll get hurt!"

All at once the driver shifted gears and the car jolted forward, leaving Craig behind.

"Goodbye," she shouted, feeling disconcerted now and unsettled, when five minutes ago she'd felt nothing but angry resolve. She turned to look out the back window and caught a haunting glimpse of him staring after her before a turn in the road cut off her view.

As she sat in a slump, biting her thumbnail half a minute later, the driver's voice distracted her. "We're coming to the end of the private road, miss. Where do you want me to take you?"

She looked up. "Oh...let me think. What's the best hotel in Kailua-Kona? Take me there." Hang the expense, she thought. Tonight she wanted only privacy and comfort. Tomorrow she'd fly home and this whole unfortunate episode of her life would be over once and for all.

8

"I've botched up everything," Jasper fretted, pacing in his hotel room after dinner. He'd observed Penelope and Craig leaving in a hurry, only moments after they'd noticed him and Bea. Apparently his son had finally seen through their disguises. But did Craig know that he had arranged for him to meet Penelope, or was he only angry at finding his father spying on him?

"I'm so embarrassed," Bea said. "It was bad enough to have to dress like that, and for such a low purpose. But then to be caught doing it—" She sighed. "Oh, well. It's over. The pieces will just have to fall where they may."

Jasper went to the phone. "I'm going to call the condo. Maybe they're there."

"What will you say?"

"I'll think of something." He dialed the number.

The phone rang and rang until Jasper finally hung up. He muttered to himself and paced some more.

"Sit down, Jasper. You're getting yourself upset and making me nervous. Remember your heart."

Jasper barely heard her, too involved in his own thoughts. "I'm considering calling Craig's house."

"You think that's a good idea right now? He looked pretty angry when they walked out of the restaurant."

"Think he'll be less angry tomorrow? Maybe the sooner I straighten things out, the better."

"How can you straighten out this situation, Jasper? We got caught. He has a right to be incensed. All you can do is apologize for both of us and hope for the best."

"I'll tell him it was my fault. I don't want him blaming you. I talked you into it."

"I could have said no," Bea said, sounding annoyed with herself. "Trying to keep you in line is like hoping to control a Great Dane with a silk leash."

Jasper bowed his head. "If I didn't have you as my conscience, I'd probably get into even worse mischief."

Bea smiled, looking wise. "Well, call Craig. Even if he's annoyed, it would be good for him to know you regret what you've done."

"Right." Jasper found the postcard with Craig's number on it and dialed. As he listened to the phone ringing, he took in a long breath for courage.

All of a sudden he heard his son's voice speaking in a rush. "Hello? Penelope?"

"No, it's Dad." Jasper raised an eyebrow. It sounded as if Penelope had left him.

"Oh." The disappointment Craig conveyed in that one word was poignant. And then his tone changed. "What the hell do you want? You haven't messed up my life enough?"

"Messed up your life?" Jasper repeated with curiosity, already forgetting that he'd called to apologize. He needed to find out what had happened.

"Don't play dumb, you conniving old coot! Throwing a woman into my life that I can't get over! Blast you! Damn you! Stay out of my business!" There was a click and then the dial tone.

Jasper smiled and hung up.

"What did he say?"

"A few things that were rather unrepeatable," he told Bea. He sat down and scratched his ear, still enjoying Craig's retort. "But he also said something very interesting—he accused me of throwing a woman in his path that he couldn't get over."

Bea's hazel eyes widened with surprise. "Maybe he *has* become attached to her. But he seems to see it as a problem."

"Yes," Jasper said, thinking. "I ought to visit him."

"When, tonight? If you couldn't find his house in the daytime, how will you find it now, after dark?"

Jasper pursed his mouth. "I'll go in the morning. But you're right, I need to get better directions." He got up and paced again. "I know—the concierge downstairs. Why didn't I think of that before? Be back in a minute."

Penelope tipped the bellman who brought her luggage to her hotel room.

"Thank you," he said. "Enjoy your stay."

Just as he took hold of the doorknob, she asked, "Is there someone at the hotel who can help me arrange flights back to the mainland? My tickets were given to me by someone else, and I find I have to change them."

"The concierge downstairs can help you with that."

She thanked him again and he left. Grabbing her handbag, she found her set of flight tickets. If she wasn't so upset right now, she'd try calling the airline herself. But there was the inter-island flight and the oceanic flight to change, and in her state of mind, it just seemed too much to handle for a novice traveler like herself. And that was the advantage of staying at a first-rate hotel—they had extra services she was paying for anyway.

When she got down to the lobby, she found the concierge's desk, but there was a man ahead of her. As she waited a polite distance away, she could hear his voice. It sounded disturbingly familiar. She looked at him again, and her heart stopped. It was Jasper. She could tell now, even from the back. There were no sunglasses or hat to mislead her.

All at once, as if he had a sixth sense, he turned around.

"Penelope!" he exclaimed with a smile.

Feeling like a deer in headlights, she tried to back away.

"No, don't go. I'm so glad I ran into you. The universe is with us!" He quickly approached, folding up what looked like a map and tucking it into his shirt pocket. "Bea and I feel terrible. Craig apparently recognized us and—"

"I don't want to talk to you, Jasper," she said, sidestepping him, finding her wits. "I know all about your matchmaking scheme. Craig told me."

"Ah, so he knows. Well, Craig may have a narrow opinion of my little attempt to play Cupid. But *I* knew you would be perfect for him."

"Thanks," she said with sarcasm, keeping her voice low, "but I don't enjoy being manipulated and tricked any more than your son does. Because of your scheming, I now feel humiliated and used—by both you and by Craig. So save your explanations and apologies. I don't want to hear them. I should have known better than to check in at the best hotel in town—naturally that's where a wealthy man like you would be staying. Which reminds me...."

Penelope stopped to rifle through her purse. She found two keys and held them out. "Take back the key to your condo. And here's the key to the rental car you arranged for me. It's there in your parking space. I'll have no more use for either.''

''What are you planning to do?'' Jasper asked, taking the keys from her with obvious reluctance.

''Go home.''

The old man looked crushed. ''But—''

''Jasper, if you say one word to try to talk me out of leaving, I swear I'll scream right here in the lobby! Your scheme didn't work. Craig and I are not now, and never will be, a pair!''

''But Bea and I saw you together, and you always looked as if you got along so well.''

''I don't want to talk about that. Our...'' She paused to try to find an appropriate word. ''Our acquaintance-ship was merely a...a convenience. In the end it amounted to nothing. Zip. I never want to see your irre-sponsible, beach-happy son again!''

''How does *he* feel?''

Penelope grew miffed that Jasper still had the nerve to ask prying questions after all she'd said. ''I have no idea! He was as looney as the Mad Hatter when I left.''

''Really? What did he say?''

''I don't remember,'' she responded with rising impa-tience. ''It made no sense, so I left.''

''You had an argument, then?''

''We both concluded that our...our friendship was over—as we both knew it would end all along. There is nothing left between us that you can use as a sign of hope, Jasper. Now I think it's time for you to find some-one else to chat with! Goodbye!'' She walked off and took a seat in front of the concierge's desk, clenching her teeth, hoping Jasper wouldn't dare persist in trying to talk to her.

"Can I help you with something?" the young woman behind the desk asked, studying Penelope's distracted expression.

"Is the elderly man you just talked to still standing behind me?"

"No," she said. "He's walking toward the elevators."

Penelope's cheeks puffed with a sigh of relief. "Thank God. I'd like you to help me get a flight off this island as early as possible in the morning. And then from Honolulu, I need to get a flight to Chicago."

"Certainly, ma'am. We'll get to work on that right now."

Jasper used the local map the concierge had marked for him last night to find his way to Craig's house. Bea had agreed to stay at the hotel. Though she wanted to see her son, she'd acquiesced to Jasper's wish to talk to Craig alone, "man to man." Jasper knew it probably wouldn't be a pretty scene, and he wanted to spare Bea the unpleasantness.

Following the route marked, Jasper turned down a narrow road with thick foliage on either side. He drove along it wondering if he was going to get himself hopelessly lost, since the road seemed to lead nowhere. And then all at once he found himself in a clearing, with an impressive two-story house in front of him surrounded by a lush lawn and tropical gardens. "For heaven's sake!" Jasper exclaimed with pleasure. "Craig's done very well for himself indeed!"

He parked and walked up to the front door. A brand new Porsche sports car sat in the carport, and he knew his son must be home.

* * *

Craig lay on the couch downstairs in the same clothes he'd worn last night. He'd never gone up to his bedroom. His whole house felt empty as a tomb. The thought of lying down alone in his king-size bed had been too painful, so he'd stayed downstairs feeling angry and bereft until he finally fell asleep on the couch. He hadn't had breakfast yet, but didn't feel like getting up to eat. God, Penelope had thrown him for a loop! No female had ever had such a disruptive effect on him. But he'd get over her, he insisted to himself. He didn't need a woman in his life!

All at once he heard a knock on his door. Maybe it was Ned. Craig didn't want his old buddy to see him this way, so he didn't get up to answer. But the knock came again, and he remembered his car was outside. He got up, running his fingers through his disheveled hair. His clothes were all rumpled, and he hadn't shaven. No doubt Ned would have some choice remarks to make.

When Craig opened his front door, he was shocked to find his father standing there. But he realized he should have expected this—Jasper had always relished having confrontations with him. Craig had survived many heated "discussions" with his directive, uncompromising dad in his youth. His shoulders slumped. He didn't know if he had the energy for more father-son combat just now.

"Hello, Craig. Hope you don't mind my stopping by like this."

"Why would you think I wouldn't mind? I told you on the phone last night to leave me be. And how the hell did you find this place?"

"I hired a private detective to locate you," Jasper replied with no apparent sense of embarrassment.

"You had a private detective snooping on me?"

"Your purchase of this house is a matter of public record, so it took only minimum effort on the gumshoe's part to glean the information. Finding out that you're a millionaire took a little more work. The detective was good at research—it was tailing you where he fell down on the job. I fired him."

"Tailing me? So that explains the white car following me." Craig glared at his father. "You ought to be ashamed of yourself! Can't you ever behave like a normal father?"

"I've never claimed to be an average person, so however you define normal probably doesn't apply to me. But just so you know—yes, I am ashamed of myself. Bea is certainly upset with my behavior. But I'm only ashamed to a certain degree. You see, you've been highly secretive yourself!"

Jasper glanced around Craig as they stood at the door, peeking into the house. "Here you are, one of the most successful men in Hawaii, the new owner of this magnificent home, yet you kept us believing that you were barely making ends meet. Your mother worries about you. After your last postcard, I decided to find out what your situation really was. And I was pleasantly surprised."

Craig clenched his jaw. "I never wanted your approval. I never wanted to be a millionaire!"

"But you are."

"It was accidental."

Jasper laughed. "Well, then, apparently you just have that magic Midas touch—like me. You're my son whether you wish to be or not. Can't change heredity. We share the same money-making gene."

Craig leaned tiredly against the door frame. He had no argument to give his father. Somewhere in his subconscious, he always knew he was a clone of his dad in many ways. He supposed he had to learn to accept that about himself.

"Since I'm here, can I see the house?"

Craig closed his eyes tightly, then relented and stepped aside, allowing his father to enter. As Jasper looked up at the beamed cathedral ceilings, murmuring in awe, then walked toward the huge windows to see the view, Craig grew restless, still out-of-sorts about his life and his feelings toward his overinfluential parent.

"You set me up, didn't you? That detective you hired knew I was having work done here. You guessed I'd have to stay at your condo, so you made sure to plant Penelope there."

"Marvelous view," Jasper said, his dark eyes bright with satisfaction. He turned to Craig. "Yes, you've pretty much figured it out. I was very lucky in my timing. I suspected you might be exiled from your home for the renovations, but I didn't know exactly when. And, of course, you might have stayed with a friend, not at my condo. But, you see, the universe was with me. My positive attitude paid off."

"The universe?" Craig said with a sardonic laugh. "Is that like the Force in *Star Wars?* What about your 'needlepoint voodoo'? Did you think my brothers wouldn't warn me? How clever to send Penelope, the very source of your war material! Had to get out the heavy artillery to try to get *me* married off, didn't you?"

"I wanted you to meet Penelope because I thought she was ideal for you. I still do. And I believe, deep in your heart, you think so, too."

"Oh? How could you possibly know my state of mind?"

"You two seemed to get along well. But my deduction about your 'state of mind'—I see you're avoiding any admission of emotion—comes from what you said last night on the phone."

Craig drew a blank. He'd been so angry at hearing his dad's voice, when he'd hoped to hear Penelope's, that he had no idea what he'd said when he chewed out his father.

Jasper seemed eager to refresh his memory. "You accused me of throwing a woman into your life that you couldn't get over."

Craig paused, vaguely remembering saying something like that. "Last night I was upset... overreacting because she'd suddenly walked out. Just injured pride—women don't usually walk out on me. But she's apparently leaving Hawaii soon, and I'll get over it."

"Oh, she's definitely gone. Probably on the flight to Honolulu as we speak."

The news hit Craig like a punch in his chest. "How do you know?"

"As I waited in front of my hotel this morning for the valet service to bring around my rental car, I saw her boarding the airport shuttle. By coincidence, she happened to come to the same hotel as Bea and I are staying at."

Craig felt as if he were sinking into the floor. "Did you talk to her?"

"Not this morning. I did run into her last night in the lobby." Jasper's expression grew regretful for the first time. "She said she felt used by both of us. She didn't want to talk to me."

Craig experienced a renewed surge of anger. "Can't you see the harm you've done?"

Jasper lowered his eyes and chewed his lower lip for a moment. "Yes, I do see. Things didn't turn out as I'd planned."

"You can't 'plan' your sons' lives! You've got no right to try to, either."

Jasper gave an innocent shrug of his shoulders. "But it worked out so well for Charles and Jake. Perhaps my success went to my head. Bea warned me you weren't like your brothers. She believes you're a confirmed bachelor."

"Well, she's right!" Craig said with emphasis. "I *do* like the single life. I'm free—don't have to consider anyone else's feelings. I can come and go without having to inform anyone. I don't have a wife to talk me out of things I'd like to do. I don't have to worry about pregnancies and—" Craig stopped, swallowing convulsively. "No rebellious kids to...drive me nuts," he added, regathering his composure.

"The rebellious kids are the best part," Jasper said with sardonic humor. His expression changed and his eyes took on a curious gleam. "Are you worried you may have gotten Penelope pregnant?"

"No!"

"Oh," Jasper said. "For a second there, I—"

"It's none of your business!"

"So, your relationship did become physical," Jasper said, the darting lights in his eyes growing even brighter.

Craig did not answer, feeling stymied. His father always had a way of winnowing out the truth. He could monitor reactions better than a lie detector. "I just told you, it's none of your damned business!"

"You're absolutely right," Jasper agreed with apparent equanimity. No wonder, Craig thought, since he'd just found out what he'd wanted to know. "So," Jasper said, rubbing his hands together, "how's business? I understand you've got a tour boat in every port!"

"Yeah," Craig said, turning away, rubbing his eyes, which burned with fatigue. "I'm doing great. You want to see my business portfolio? Be my guest."

"I would," Jasper said with interest. "But not now. You...look tired. Actually you look like you've been run over by a dump truck."

Craig tugged up his belt and pushed falling hair off his forehead. "Fell asleep on the couch last night," he muttered.

"Losing the love of your life will do that," Jasper said matter-of-factly.

"She's not the—"

"No?"

"No!"

"If you say so." Jasper's tone was airy now. "Well, I guess I ought to be going, so you can shave and so on. You probably have plans for the day."

Jasper's sudden decision to leave took Craig by surprise. "I'll...see you to the door."

As they walked toward the front door together, Craig felt guilty about his mom. "How long will you be on the island?"

"I've been thinking maybe we should leave tomorrow. I've got a condo on Maui, and Bea would probably enjoy a stay there. She feels we're intruding on you, just being on the same island."

Craig took a long breath. "I'm free this afternoon. Why don't you bring her over?"

Jasper's eyes widened. "Really? She would enjoy seeing this house, you know. I haven't told her anything. She still assumes you're in some little fixer-upper somewhere."

This news puzzled Craig. "Why didn't you tell her what you learned from that detective?"

"Because I thought she should hear about your success from you. If I tell her, then she'll know you've been hiding the truth from us, and she'll be disappointed. If you tell her, then it will seem more like a wonderful surprise."

Craig felt low now for having deceived his mom. "You're right. Bring her over this afternoon, after lunch. It's time to end *my* charade."

"Good," Jasper said. "Your mother will be very relieved. Want to have lunch with us?"

"No." Craig's stomach felt like it was twisted in a knot. "Just come here when you've finished eating."

Jasper left in a good frame of mind.

After showering and shaving, Craig spent the next few hours tidying up the kitchen and straightening up the bedroom. While smoothing the bedspread, he tried not to think about the passion he'd shared with Penelope or the contented sleep he'd always experienced with her lying next to him. He tried to keep his mind on his mother and on finally making her happy to be his mom. For decades he'd been his parents' primary source of grief.

Around two, Jasper's rental car pulled up to the house again. Craig went out to greet them, giving his mother a bear hug.

"It's so nice to see you and be able to *talk* to you," Bea told him. "Jasper always had to restrain me."

"I hardly recognize you without your hat and sunglasses," he teased her.

"I've thrown them away!" Bea said with a wave of her hand. "I'll never wear them again."

"The loud shirts, too?" he said, eyeing her delicate pink blouse.

"Those, too, though Jasper seems to want to hang on to his."

"It was fun dressing boldly," Jasper said with a chuckle. "I've been too conservative all my life."

"Only in your wardrobe, dear," Bea said. She turned to look at the house. "Golly, Craig, is this really your home? I couldn't believe it when we pulled up and Jasper said this was the place."

Craig assured her with pride that he did indeed own the house. He took her inside and showed her every room. She oohed and ahed with childlike excitement, exclaiming over the view, the large proportions of the rooms, the beauty of the wood floors and woodwork, and the grand staircase. Craig got out his business portfolio, and actually took pleasure in seeing Jasper suitably impressed. When Bea looked confused by the complex numbers, Jasper explained to her that Craig was a millionaire. This brought tears to Bea's eyes.

"A millionaire? Well, I guess I don't need to worry how you're doing anymore. I was afraid you had gotten in over your head buying this house, but apparently not!"

"I got it for a steal," Craig told her. "Well within my budget, which seems to grow bigger every year. Actually, my accountant informed me last week that some investments paid off and I'm worth seven million now."

"You've got a prospering business you're obviously committed to," Jasper said in a complimentary tone of voice. "Isn't it about time you made a commitment to share your life—and this huge house—with a woman? Especially now that you've met the ideal woman?"

"Jasper," Bea chided, "don't start—"

"I agree with Mom," Craig said. "We're getting along nicely for a change. Don't start up with me again."

"Okay. All right," Jasper said. "Just thought I'd make the point. Now it's made. We can move on."

"Would you like some tea?" Craig asked his mother. "I've got a box of cookies stashed away."

"That would be lovely," Bea said.

Craig went into the kitchen to start some water boiling. When he came out, he found his parents in the living room, looking it over from different angles, remarking on the beauty of the view again.

"How are you going to decorate it?" Bea asked.

Craig felt deflated by the question. "I don't know. I need to hire a decorator, I guess." He remembered Penelope's imaginative description of how she'd do the room, and he suddenly felt very lonely again.

"What's this?" Bea asked, picking up a plastic bag from the space between the sofa and the wall. "Oh..." she said as she read the writing on the plastic.

"What is it?" Craig asked. He hadn't known anything was in that corner and had missed it during his cleanup.

Bea handed it to him without a word.

Craig blinked as he read Penelope's Needlepoint Shop scrolled across the bag in bold calligraphy. He looked inside and took out the needlepoint piece—a woman with a unicorn—he'd seen her working on in quiet moments on the couch. "She must have left it," Craig said. "She...packed in a hurry."

Bea took the square, nearly finished canvas from him. "She once told me she liked Medieval designs. This is taken from a section of a famous French tapestry. She's done a beautiful job on it."

Craig's hands felt cold and stiff. "Maybe you should take it back to her."

His mother's expression grew troubled. "Jasper tells me she's very angry with us now. I'd be too embarrassed to see her. Perhaps you should mail it to her. The shop's address is printed on the bag."

"Her phone number is there, too," Jasper added.

"I'm not calling her." Craig took the needlepoint from his mom and stuffed it back in the bag. He tossed it on the couch. "I'll mail it. The water must be hot now. Why don't you come into the kitchen?"

When Craig fumbled with the teapot, still disconcerted at finding Penelope's needlework, Bea took over and made the tea. They sat down at the kitchen table. Bea poured and Jasper opened up the box of store-bought cookies.

"You seem upset," Bea said gently, looking concerned.

"No, I'm fine."

"He's just in love," Jasper said.

"I'm *not* in love," Craig insisted with impatience. "I'm not in love!"

Jasper merely smiled at his protests.

"Leave him alone," Bea said. "He must figure out things on his own. We gave him the problem, but he has to solve it. Don't shove answers down his throat, Jasper."

"Of course, Bea." Jasper patted her hand. "You're always right about these things. You'd be a far better matchmaker than me if you put your mind to it."

"One in the family is more than enough," Bea said, giving Jasper a severe look.

Craig couldn't help but grow amused despite his inner turmoil. His parents had been like this for as long as he could remember. Their commitment to each other had always been strong enough to weather their differences of

opinion and temperament. Craig wondered—doubted—
if he could be that committed to one woman for the rest
of his life. He didn't know if he had that kind of staying
power.

Eventually his parents left, sharing hugs all around on
Craig's doorstep.

"I hope it won't be another two years before we see
you again," Bea said.

Craig wanted to promise that he'd fly to Chicago to see
them, but then he remembered Penelope lived there and
knew the temptation to see her would be too great.
"You'll have to come back to the island," he told his
mom. "By the way, I thought you didn't like to fly. How
did Dad manage to get you here?"

"Penelope told her about wristbands for motion sickness," Jasper said eagerly. "Bea tried them and they
worked."

Craig nodded at the explanation, wishing Penelope's
name hadn't come up again. Jasper still wasn't missing
any opportunities.

He found his father studying him. "Aren't your feelings for her stronger than your need to rebel against
me?" Jasper asked, as if giving it one last try. "Just because I chose her, doesn't mean you should reject her."

"No, it's not that," Craig said. "Not anymore. I never
wanted to get married, that's all."

"Never is a long time," the old man said.

After they left, Jasper's parting words kept rattling
around Craig's brain. In the evening, he sat on the couch
looking at Penelope's needlework. He remembered how
she'd talked about tapestries she'd hang on his walls that
would take a lifetime to make. If they were as detailed
and finely textured as the one in his hands, what quality
and warmth they would add to the bare walls that sur-

rounded him. Like his mother, she had an appreciation for artistic and romantic things.

She was too classy for a reformed beach bum like him, Craig thought, finding a new reason to forget her. She probably wouldn't marry him even if he did ask. Except that she had expressed love for him, in words and in the sweetness of her embrace, in the tender way she'd made love. No woman had ever moved him to tears before. Penelope was as unusual as her name.

He got up and went to a bookshelf in his bedroom, half filled with books he'd kept from college. In a moment he found the one he was searching for—a book of mythology from a literature class. He looked under Greek mythology and found the paragraph on Odysseus' wife, Penelope. Craig read the legend, which he'd forgotten.

Odysseus had been gone from Ithaca for twenty years. During his long absence, when it was thought he would never return, his lonely wife Penelope was set upon by numerous suitors who wished to marry her. But Penelope always hoped for Odysseus's return, so she found a way to gain time and put off her admirers. She promised to choose one of her suitors once she finished a certain piece of weaving. Each night, however, she would undo the stitches she'd woven during the day—which explained the origin of the term *Penelope's Web*: anything that is perpetually under way and never completed. Her methodology worked. When Odysseus eventually returned, he slew all her suitors.

Good for him, Craig thought as he closed the book. And then he realized how sophomoric he was being, looking up Penelope's name in a book like some adolescent with a crush. He realized he hadn't stopped thinking about her for one moment since she'd left. Would he ever get her out of his mind? He felt as if he'd gotten caught in an invisible web she'd stitched around him. Would he ever be free?

She'd only been gone a day. He needed time, that was all, he assured himself. He'd forget her—and soon.

Craig returned to his office and threw himself back into work. Weeks went by. He ignored Ned's pointed barbs and insisted that he was over Penelope. The busy tourist season helped keep his mind occupied. He worked late instead of delegating projects to his employees.

But when he did come home, his house was still bare and empty. He continued to have a hard time falling asleep. And he never mailed the needlepoint piece to Chicago.

One day when he was at the office working late, Ned stopped by.

"You still here?" Ned asked. "You're turning into a workaholic!"

"Just had some paperwork to finish. What's up?"

Ned handed him a small newspaper clipping. "You got your name in the paper."

Craig read it and exhaled with impatience. He'd donated money to an environmental group whose aim was to protect Hawaii's undersea fish and flora. But he'd thought he'd made it clear to the organization that he wanted his donation to be kept quiet.

"Great," he muttered. "I was supposed to be anonymous."

"No harm in looking like a good guy," Ned said. "Tidy sum of money, too!"

"Now that everyone knows I've got dollars to spare for causes, every charity will be after me." He tucked the clipping into his wallet, intending to ask the organization how his name had gotten leaked to the press.

"Yeah," Ned said with a mocking sigh, "it must be rough to be so rich. How's your love life?"

"Back to normal," Craig said, taking a blithe tone.

"Normal? So you're living like a hermit again?"

"I'm doing fine."

Ned sat on the corner of Craig's desk. "You know, boss, it's not going to wash. Everyone has noticed that you're distracted, you're uncharacteristically short-tempered, you work constantly and you're not eating well. The gossip is that you fell in love and lost the girl."

Craig's jaw tightened. He wanted to insist that he wasn't in love, but somehow he couldn't tell Ned that as forthrightly as he used to.

"Why do people assume that?" Craig asked, keeping his eyes lowered.

"Because you were seen all over the island with her, and you even took time off from work, apparently to spend it with her. Now the lady seems to have disappeared, and you're acting like a bear and working fourteen hours a day. You think people can't read between the lines?"

"I just wish they'd spend their time doing something other than reading."

"Get real! The world runs on gossip. But if you marry her, you'll be old news once the wedding's over and everyone will find new fodder."

"Now there's the best reason to get married I've heard yet!"

"You still think bachelorhood is the way to go?" Ned asked. "Look at you—you're a mess! A grown man turned into a basket case. If you need that lady in your life, quit sitting behind that desk. Get off your duff and do something about it!"

Craig glared at him.

Ned responded by pointing a finger back at him. "I'm giving you the best advice you'll ever get. And I don't care if you fire me!"

9

—◆—

Penelope ripped out the incorrect stitches she'd made on the new project she was working on, a sleeping unicorn taken from a sixteenth-century tapestry. She wondered how she had lost the nearly finished companion piece she'd taken with her to Hawaii, though she shouldn't be surprised, considering her state of mind the night she left Craig. Confused, hysterical, panicked—words had seemed inadequate to describe her feelings. And on top of all that, she'd still had a nagging fear that she might be pregnant, learning the nerve-racking way that careless sex had its risks.

But the day after she got home her period had started, thank God. She'd never repeat *that* mistake. Now she could forget it all, she'd told herself. She could get over her whole interlude with Craig—all the passion, and all the heartache.

But little things kept obsessing her—like her lost needlework. Had she dropped it at one of the airports, or had she left it at Craig's house? If it was at Craig's house, what would he do with it when he found it? Would he think she'd left it on purpose, so he would have to contact her about it? Weeks had gone by and she hadn't heard from him. But that was good, she insisted to herself.

She looked out the window of her store to see if there were any customers on their way, but the whole shopping center was quiet today. Everyone must be taking an August vacation, she thought, sighing with impatience as she worked at loosening the tight stitches. How had she sewn it wrong in the first place? Ever since she'd returned, her mind hadn't been able to focus on the present. At first she'd cried a lot, but she'd soon decided that wouldn't do any good. Then she'd begun to work hard at suppressing every thought of Craig. For several days it seemed to work. At least, she'd stopped crying. But then her mind seemed to grow even more fuzzy. She started dreaming about him every night.

Yesterday she'd had an even more unsettling indication that all was not well with her emotionally. It was Sunday and her store was closed. To try to raise her spirits, she'd gone downtown to North Michigan Avenue to shop. In a department store she'd come upon a display of Venetian glass paperweights. She found one that depicted colorful tropical fish swimming over multicolored sand amid green strings of seaweed. All at once she burst into tears and had to leave the store.

How silly! What was wrong with her? When was she going to get over Craig? Apparently suppressing thoughts of him wasn't doing her any good, either, if he was popping up in sensual dreams and if she couldn't look at a paperweight without dissolving into tears. Perhaps she should do just the opposite and think about him all the time—until she got sick of it. She'd been trying that method all day today. But she was finding, unfortunately, that she cherished reliving every memory.

Grimacing as she fought with a stitch bound up too tightly to loosen and pull out, she glanced up when she heard the door open. Finally a customer—

She saw Craig standing a few feet away, studying her with curious eyes. The needle and canvas dropped from her hands onto the countertop.

"Craig!" She couldn't believe her eyes.

"Working on a new one?" he asked. He picked it up. "Are you actually undoing stitches? Amazing. Well, you can stop now—Odysseus has returned."

"W-what are you doing here?" she asked, ignoring his nonsensical chatter. His sudden unexpected presence discombobulated her. She almost wondered if she was hallucinating from thinking about him too much. When she noticed his clothes, she was even more convinced her imagination was running amuck. He was wearing a tie and a lightweight pale gray jacket that was beautifully tailored. Where had he gotten such clothes? And why?

"I flew in last night. I wanted to see you...see how you are," he replied, looking terribly serious now.

"I'm not pregnant, if that's what you're worried about," she rushed to assure him. "My monthly cycle went on as usual."

He looked down. With a little smile, he said, "Maybe we'll have better luck next time."

Next time? "What do you mean?"

He seemed at a loss for words and looked away, running his fingertips along his nose. "I'm not good at this. I never expected to find myself in this situation..."

"What situation?" she asked. "Why are you here? I never expected to see you again. I didn't *want* to ever see you again." A thought came to her—had there been a serious illness or a death in his family? Had he flown to Chicago for a funeral? "Are your parents okay?"

The question seemed to distract him. "I think so," he replied with a shrug. "I haven't been to see them yet. I came to see you."

"But *why?*"

"I've...thought about it a lot, and...I want to marry you."

Her tense shoulders rose upward. She felt a buzzing sensation in her brain. "Oh, God, Craig. Are you crazy?"

"Well, yeah. I'm crazy in love—with you. Nothing's been the same since you left. I can't sleep, I've lost weight, I work constantly, but nothing changes. I can't get myself back to normal. The house is so empty. My whole damn life feels empty. I need you sharing my space or I'm not happy."

"My life isn't normal anymore, either," she told him, anger showing in her tone, "but it would be a bad solution to get married. Things would only get worse."

His eyebrows drew together and he leaned over the counter. She felt a bit overwhelmed as he looked her in the eye. "Why would they get worse?" he asked.

"Because you...you're like my father, a smooth-talking guy who can't hold down a job and makes promises he can't keep."

"Your father?" He raised his forefinger as if remembering. "That's right, you mentioned your parents were unhappily married. But that doesn't mean it'll be the same with us."

"No? Your idea of a job is house-sitting. You're working constantly!" She laughed, repeating what he'd just told her. "Doing what? Dusting? Turning off the lights at night?"

Craig rubbed his brow. "This is why truth is always the best policy. I shouldn't have let you believe..." He paused and looked at her again. "I'm not house-sitting, Penelope. I own the house."

She narrowed her gaze at him. "You own it?"

"I can show you the deed, if you want to see it. But what I own or don't own, what my financial situation is, isn't important. It's how we feel—"

"How can you say that? Of course it's important."

His mouth and eyes grew firm. "I want you to put that aside for right now and tell me something—and I want you to be honest. Do you love me?"

She looked down at her hands on the counter. Tears started in her eyes and she didn't reply.

"You said that you loved me. I know it was in a moment of passion, but...I believed it. I don't think you lied when you said it. I think your words came from your heart."

She wiped away the tears now streaming down her face. "Of course, I love you!" she replied. "But that's a stupid reason to get married."

"Stupid?" he said, raising his voice slightly. "It's the best of all reasons!"

"Don't you see it can't last?"

"No! I love you, too. Why can't it last?"

"We haven't known each other long, for one thing. My mother married in a hurry, afraid she'd lose the man she'd fallen for. When it became clear he couldn't support her and their child—" she pointed to herself "—everything started falling apart. He lied, always promising to do better, he cheated on her, and finally he left. He ruined her life."

With determination Craig stepped around the counter and took her by the shoulders. He shook her a bit as he said, "I am not your father!"

"You're just like him!"

"I love you and I'll take care of you."

"No," she said, new tears streaming down her face. "I'll wind up supporting *you*. And God knows how I'd do that. Does Kailua-Kona need a needlepoint shop? I'd probably have to start selling T-shirts or something."

Craig shook his head adamantly. "You can work if you want, but you wouldn't have to. You can spend your time decorating our house, if you want. You can spend time with our children."

She had to laugh at that. "You want to be a father?"

He made a self-conscious grin. "The idea's beginning to interest me, oddly enough. If you're their mom, I think I could adjust to having little kids running up to me, calling me Daddy, when I come home from work."

He looked and sounded so sincere, she wanted to believe him. But she knew that would be a mistake. "What work would you come home from?"

"At . . . the office."

"What office?"

He exhaled, as if feeling pulled in more than one direction. "I'll tell you about all that later. First, I want to know if you'll marry me."

"No."

He gripped her shoulders more firmly. "But you love me."

"Yes. But I won't marry you."

The disappointment on his face cut her in two. "Then will you come back to Hawaii and live with me?"

"Live with you?"

"Share my house and my life."

"Oh, Craig," she said, shaking her head. The idea was tempting, to be with him but not be legally tied to him. "I know I slept with you too easily, but I'm really sort of Victorian in my approach to life. I wouldn't feel right living with you on a long-term basis."

"I wouldn't, either," he agreed. "It would show we don't have enough faith in our future together to make it legal. And what if you got pregnant? I want my kids to have my last name, too.''

''Of course,'' she told him. ''It's the only way people should have children.''

''Okay,'' he said, ''so we've decided that if we're going to be together, then we need to be married. Right? Is this logical?''

''Nothing about dealing with you has been logical,'' she said. ''All you had to do was kiss me on that boat, and I lost track of what was sensible.''

He studied her with brightening eyes. ''All right. Maybe I should try that approach again,'' he said, sliding his hands to her waist and pulling her toward him.

''No,'' she objected, weakly trying to twist away. But when he pulled her body against his, she melted. ''Don't,'' she said in a swooning tone as his hand warmly cupped the side of her breast and his mouth lowered to hers. When their lips met, her knees grew shaky and her eyes closed in ecstasy. She had no willpower at all, some part of her brain chided her. She was a mindless wanton, born to make the same stupid mistakes her mother had always warned her about. But the strength of the passion she felt in his embrace, the potential that hung between them for reliving the blissful fulfillment he'd given her before, made her begin to doubt the value of her own common sense.

''I love you,'' he murmured in a husky voice as he kissed her neck and stroked her body. ''I want you. You've got to marry me—can't you see we were meant to be together?''

''Nothing is meant to be,'' she said, squirming in tortured pleasure at his caresses. ''People just make foolish choices, and then they have to face the consequences.''

He stopped kissing her. "What foolish choice are you going to make?"

She closed her eyes tightly and pressed her forehead against his chin. "I don't know. It's not fair to pressure me with hot kisses and caresses—you know I'm weak that way. You know I can't resist."

"Then don't resist. Tell me you'll marry me. Please— say it!"

Her fingers clenched his lapel as she leaned her head into his shoulder. She was about to make the biggest mistake of her life. Maybe it would end unhappily, but . . . she loved him. He'd even said he loved her. She'd never thought she'd hear him say that. Maybe there was some little smidgeon of hope for them.

"I'll marry you," she whispered.

He laughed with joy and hugged her so tightly, she couldn't breathe. "You won't regret it!" he promised. "I'll do my best to make you happy."

They kissed and held on to each other for a long moment. Penelope closed her eyes and clung to him, feeling mentally numb now that she'd agreed to be his wife. Emotionally, she felt jubilant and relieved from the anguish of missing him the past few weeks.

"How soon can you sell this store?" he asked her, as if getting his mind geared up to make instant plans.

"Sell it? Gosh, I don't know. I'd have to find a buyer and—"

"A real estate broker can help you with that. My dad probably has connections, so it won't be a problem. Should we get married here or in Hawaii?"

"My mom's in Florida, so she'd have to fly somewhere in either case. I guess it doesn't make any difference to me."

"How about Hawaii? You can fly back with me now and we wouldn't have to be apart again. I need to go back tomorrow. It's the busy tourist season, and I shouldn't have left."

"So you can take people out on your catamaran?" she asked.

He took her by the shoulders and held her away from him, apparently so he could see her face. His expression was tentative, yet playful with humor. "My fleet of catamarans, Penelope. Actually, I own a whole company with lots of employees, a headquarters office building, and boats in every harbor on all the islands."

"You do?" she said, her back straightening. What line was he giving her now? And why?

"I see you're doubtful. And I can understand why, because I let you believe what my parents had told you about me, what they had believed until recently. The truth is—" he looked down and seemed embarrassed "—I'm a millionaire."

"A millionaire!" she exclaimed, backing away from him.

He stepped forward, still holding on to her. "I know it's a shock. It was to me, too, when I first found out," he assured her. "It bothered me a lot. I didn't want my dad to know I'd become successful, because I didn't want to give him the satisfaction. So I kept it a secret from my parents."

Penelope was feeling faint. Was this the truth, or was Craig experiencing delusions of grandeur? She'd doubted his sanity the day she left. Maybe he *was* crazy.

"But my dad got suspicious," Craig continued, talking rapidly, "and found out my true status. I guess he thought it was time I got married, and that's when he brought you into the picture. And the rest you know."

Penelope swallowed, unsure what to think.

He studied her face closely. "You look a little pale. Is that all right with you, that you'll be marrying a millionaire?"

"If this is true," she said, wetting her lips, "why didn't you tell me before?"

He sighed, as if with regret. "Because I thought of you at first as a friend of my dad's. If you found out I was wealthy, I was afraid you'd tell him. He came to see me after you left. I was angry about his matchmaking scheme, but after some unpleasant arguing, things began to straighten out. I never thought I'd want to be married, but I've finally realized that you're the last and most important piece missing from my life. I have a rewarding career, I have a house, and I'm finally on good terms with my parents. But, much as I hated to admit it, my dad was right—I need a wife. I never thought I'd fall in love with the woman my father chose for me, but I did."

She stared at him numbly, feeling hopelessly confused by his eager explanations. "Why?"

He lifted his shoulders whimsically. "I guess I wanted a girl just like the girl that married dear old Dad," he said with a smile. "In my beach days, I met lots of babes and lots of chicks. Some of them were pretty hot. And that was fine, because all I was looking for was fun. You were different. At first I thought you were just a curiosity, but I underestimated you. You were the most adorable woman I ever saw. And you fell in love with me. When you said that, it blew my mind. I knew you were too good for me—just like my mother is too good for my dad. But somehow she has the patience to put up with him, and I'm hoping you have the patience to put up with me.

So . . . there you have it, my life in a nutshell up to this minute."

He paused and studied her again. Penelope's mind was whirling and she didn't know what to say.

"Are you okay?" he asked.

"I . . . I think so."

"You aren't saying much."

She'd already said yes to his marriage proposal. What more did he want? "What should I say?"

"That you're happy?"

"Well, gosh, Craig, you come in here suddenly, tell me you love me, ask me to marry you, and then you tell me you're a millionaire. I've never had this sort of information thrown at me so quickly before."

"You poor thing," he said, taking her in his arms again. "I have thrown a lot at you. I've had all this on my mind for weeks. I finally realized there was no use fighting it, I had to marry you. Being a confirmed bachelor had gotten pretty miserable. So I flew in and had to wait until morning to come here, since I don't know where you live. Thank God you didn't decide to take the day off," he said, kissing her forehead.

Being close in his arms again comforted her, though what he'd told her still mystified her. "I did have the day off yesterday. I went shopping and saw a paperweight with tropical fish. It made me cry because it reminded me of you."

"Did it?" he murmured as he stroked her back. "How do you think I've felt looking at your needlepointed lady and unicorn every night?"

She glanced up. "You have it?"

"Yup. I should have brought it along, but then I thought why bother if I'm going to be bringing you back with me?"

"Pretty sure of yourself," she said, touching his chin.

"No. I was scared to death you wouldn't marry me. After the way we parted, I was afraid you'd still hate me."

She shook her head. "I was upset with myself for falling in love with you."

"You aren't still upset, are you?" he asked, peering into her eyes. "You don't look quite happy yet."

"Craig, it's hard to be sure of you. You misled me when you pretended to be poor—or else you're misleading me now by claiming you have a going business and that you're a millionaire. How did you have all that time on your hands, if you had work responsibilities?"

"When you came to live with me, I took a vacation from the office. I made time to be with you. Remember at the condo, the morning after we'd made love the first time, when I had to leave in a hurry? I had a staff meeting to lead. My employees were surprised to see me come in late. I'm a stickler about promptness."

Penelope remembered that day and her heart began to beat faster. Could it be true? "What about those times in stores and restaurants when things were suddenly half price or free? Did you have something to do with that?"

He grinned. "I told Sophie on the sly to charge you half price and I reimbursed her later. I wanted you to have those outfits, and I didn't want you worrying about your budget. And at the Italian restaurant, the owner and I go way back. I've directed a lot of tourists to his place, so he always gives me dinner on the house." He bowed his head. "I hated all those times you looked at me as if you thought I was some starving homeless person, because I didn't seem to have a place to live. I wanted to level with you, but I had that hang-up about my father. I'm sorry."

"Do you have a business card?"

"Sure," he said, letting go of her to get out his wallet. The wallet was of fine, thin leather and expensive-looking. When he opened it, he apparently didn't notice a slip of paper fall to the floor. She stooped to pick it up.

"Here," he said.

She took his business card, printed on linen stock. His name was listed as CEO and President of Sunshine Snorkeling Cruises, a name she'd seen recommended in tourist pamphlets she'd found in her hotel room that last night. "That's you?"

"That's me."

She handed the card back to him and then opened up the folded paper he'd dropped, a newspaper clipping. "What's this?"

"Oh, that's just…" He seemed embarrassed. "One of my employees cut that out for me. I should throw it away."

"You donated *a hundred thousand dollars* to… Oh, my God…" Her voice trailed off in disbelief.

"I didn't expect it to be printed up in the paper for people to make a fuss over," Craig said.

Penelope began to laugh, and soon found herself in tears. Yet her laughing didn't stop.

"What's wrong?" he asked, taking her elbow.

"Sorry," she said, wiping her eyes. "I'm just feeling a little hysterical. I thought I'd wind up supporting you."

"You will," he told her. "Not financially. But you'll be the wind in my sails. You *will* be happy, Penelope. Believe it or not."

"I'm beginning to believe it," she said, sniffing, blinking hard. "Gosh. How did I get so lucky?"

"I'm the lucky one. How about lunch? I think you ought to eat something—you still look a little pale. And then we'll come back here and start closing down your shop."

She looked around at her shop, not unhappy at the prospect of giving it up. "I was in such a rut here. You've opened up a whole new world for me. I *am* happy, Craig. I'm so happy I can hardly stand it."

They kissed with affection and tenderness. And then Craig said, "My parents will be thrilled. Except I think my dad forgot something in all his machinations to get us together."

"What?"

"He'd lose this shop, the source of his voodoo techniques."

"That's right," Penelope said. "Poor Jasper."

Craig grinned. "My mom will be *so* relieved."

A month later Craig and Penelope were married in their home high above Kealakekua Bay. Penelope had selected furniture and Craig pulled strings to have it delivered in time for the wedding. A caterer helped with the decorations and the dinner. Penelope's mother was there, as well as Craig's principal employees, his parents, and his brothers, Charles and Jake, and their families.

When the ceremony, which took place on the lawn, was over and toasts were being said before dinner, Jasper rose to speak. He proudly showed everyone the wedding pillow he'd made to commemorate the occasion, pointing out that he'd stitched Penelope's and Craig's names before they'd ever met. Penelope laughed along with Bea and everyone else as his three sons gave him the raspberries.

Late that night, when everyone had left and Craig and Penelope were alone in bed, she said, "Jasper should be content now that he's got his sons all married off."

186 ME? MARRY YOU?

"Not quite. Charles and Jake have produced grandchildren. He wants us to procreate, too, and the more the better. So," Craig said, squeezing her hand, "maybe we ought to work on carrying out our obligation to the family, now that you're officially a Derring."

She raised an eyebrow. "You mean, what was pure pleasure before is going to be a duty now?"

His chuckle was low and sexy. "Forget duty. Let's go for ecstasy. Between you and me, it's never been any other way. We'd better not change anything, just because we're married."

"No, no changes," she whispered with a languid smile as she lay back on the pillow. "Everything from now on will be copacetic."

* * * * *

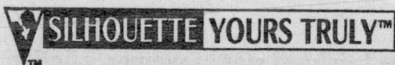

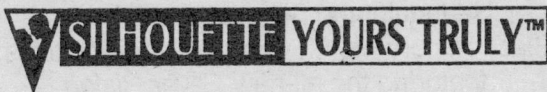

In February, Silhouette Books is proud
to present the sweeping, sensual new novel
by bestselling author

CAIT LONDON

about her unforgettable family—*The Tallchiefs*.

TALLCHIEF FOR KEEPS

Everyone in Amen Flats, Wyoming, was talking about
Elspeth Tallchief. How she wasn't a thirty-three-year-old
virgin, after all. How she'd been keeping herself warm at
night all these years with a couple of secrets. And now one
of those secrets had walked right into town, sending
everyone into a frenzy. But Elspeth knew he'd come for
the *other* secret....

"Cait London is an irresistible storyteller…"
—*Romantic Times*

Don't miss TALLCHIEF FOR KEEPS by Cait London, available
at your favorite retail outlet in February from

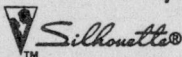